TIME TRAVEL
TW

THE

ROMAN

INVASION

TIME TRAVEL
TWINS

THE
ROMAN
INVASION

JOSH LACEY
ILLUSTRATED BY GARRY PARSONS

ANDERSEN PRESS

First published in Great Britain in 2023 by
Andersen Press Limited
20 Vauxhall Bridge Road, London SW1V 2SA, UK
Vijverlaan 48, 3062 HL Rotterdam, Nederland
www.andersenpress.co.uk

2 4 6 8 10 9 7 5 3 1

British Library Cataloguing in Publication Data available.

ISBN 978 1 83913 334 3

Printed and bound in Great Britain by Clays Ltd, Elcograf S.p.A.

Look out for more in the
Time Travel Twins series!

Time Travel Twins: The Viking Attack

1

'Could you lay the table, please?' Mum asked. 'Lunch will be ready in ten minutes.'

Reluctantly Thomas got to his feet, collected a handful of cutlery from the drawer and set out five places. Scarlett fetched some glasses and filled a jug with cold water.

It was Saturday, and the twins and their parents had brought lunch to their

grandfather's house: lasagne, garlic bread and salad, to be followed by chocolate pudding and vanilla ice cream.

Mum was worried that Grandad wasn't eating properly.

Grandad had always been a bit of a mess. His clothes were dirty, his hair stuck up all over the place, and he often forgot to shower or shave, but recently he had been looking even scruffier than usual, and he appeared to have lost weight.

'You're not getting any younger,' Mum reminded him. 'You need to look after yourself.'

Grandad told her not to make a fuss, he was fine, he was just working so hard that he didn't have time for showering, shaving or washing his clothes.

'Or eating?' Mum asked.

'Sometimes I forget,' Grandad admitted.

Right now, Grandad was in his workshop, doing some more work before lunch.

He lived in a quiet forest, more than a mile from the nearest neighbour. Opposite his house was a large barn, which he had converted into his workshop.

Mum looked out of the kitchen window at the closed door of Grandad's workshop. A handwritten notice warned in big letters:

DANGER
DO NOT ENTER

'I wish I knew what he was doing in there,' Mum said. 'When is he going to tell us?'

Thomas and Scarlett gave one another a glance.

Mum noticed. 'Has he told you?' she asked.

Thomas shook his head. 'No, Mum.'

'He says it's a secret,' Scarlett added.

Mum sighed. 'I don't know why he has to be so mysterious. He won't even allow me past the doorway. He promised he'd tell me what he's doing as soon as he can, but he's been saying that for years.'

Thomas and Scarlett nodded, and tried to look as if neither of them had any idea what Grandad might be working on. They felt bad about lying to their mother, but they were in a difficult position. Their grandfather had sworn them to secrecy, so they either had to break their promise to him, or lie to their mother. Both options were bad, obviously, but which was worse?

Once Thomas and Scarlett had laid the table, and their parents had made the salad, they were ready to eat.

Mum said. 'Can one of you go and get Grandad?'

'I'll go,' Thomas said.

'Shall I come too?' Scarlett asked, but her brother had already gone.

Scarlett returned to her book and continued turning the pages, learning about the Roman empire, looking at pictures of Roman senators in long white flowing robes and the extraordinary architecture of ancient Rome: the circus, the temples, the forum, the catacombs and the Colosseum.

She and Thomas were studying the Romans at school. Their teacher, Miss Wellington, had asked them to research some facts over the weekend about Boudicca, the British queen who had fought back against the Romans.

Scarlett was so absorbed in her reading that she didn't even notice how much time had passed, but a few minutes must have gone by because she was snapped out of reverie by her mother saying, 'What on earth is taking them so long?'

'I'll go over there and give them a shout,' Dad said.

'I'll do it.' Scarlett put a bookmark between the pages of her book, and hurried out of the room. She left the house, crossed the yard and entered the workshop, ignoring the sign pinned on the door. She saw her grandfather and her brother standing beside the enormous machine which took up most of the workshop. This was the project which had occupied many years of Grandad's life.

'Lunch is ready,' Scarlett said.

'Give us a minute,' Grandad replied.

Scarlett realised immediately what was going on. She couldn't believe it. 'What do you think you're doing?' she asked her twin brother.

'I would have thought you'd be pleased,' Thomas replied. 'You're always saying I should care more about history.'

'I wish you did care more about history,'

Scarlett said. 'But this isn't the right moment
to research the Romans. Lunch is ready. Mum's
about to take the lasagne out of the oven.'

'This is a time machine, dumbo.'

'That's not a nice way to talk to your sister,'
Grandad said.

'Sorry,' Thomas said. 'But I'm right, aren't
I? When I come back to the present, no time
will have passed. Mum will still be taking the
lasagne out of the oven.' Thomas nodded to

his grandfather. 'Let's go, Grandad. I'm ready when you are.'

'I'm coming too,' Scarlett blurted out without thinking.

'I thought we didn't have time for this?' Thomas said.

'We don't,' Scarlett replied. 'But I'm not letting you go without me.'

She kicked off her shoes. Her T-shirt and shorts might look a bit strange to anyone living in the past, but her trainers would look utterly extraordinary so it was better to leave them in the present. Thomas was barefoot already.

Grandad fixed a tiny transmitter to the back of Scarlett's front teeth, and inserted a little translator into her right ear. Thomas was already wearing identical devices. Now they could understand and speak any language that had ever been spoken on Earth.

'You'd better not forget these,' Grandad said. He handed each of them a device about the size of a phone. When you pressed the button in the middle of the device, you would be returned to the present, where not a single second would have passed.

Grandad had explained the workings of the time machine to both Thomas and Scarlett, but neither of them had understood him very well. The explanations involved quantum mechanics, theoretical physics and a lot of complicated equations. What they did understand was this: the time machine activated a wormhole, which somehow connected together two different points in time and space, so you could travel between them as easily as walking from one room to another.

Even Grandad wasn't quite sure how it actually worked, and he said the wormhole seemed to have a mind of its own, so the results of the time machine weren't always exactly what he was expecting.

'I've given each of you one of these devices in case you're separated,' he said. 'Obviously it would be safer if you stayed together, but you never know what might happen.'

Thomas and Scarlett carefully placed the devices in their pockets. Once they had stepped into the time machine, that device was the only way that they could get home.

'What year are you going back to?' Grandad asked the children.

'Don't ask me,' Thomas said. He turned to his sister. 'When did Boudicca live?'

'You should listen to Miss Wellington,' Scarlett told her brother. 'You might learn something.'

'Very funny. Come on, tell me. When was it?'

'Boudicca fought the Romans in the year sixty-one,' Scarlett replied.

'Perfect. Let's see. If I go all the way back to zero,' Grandad mumbled to himself as he turned the dial on the time machine. 'Then to fifty. Sixty. Sixty-one. There you go.'

He clicked the main switch from OFF to ON. A low hum filled the air. Some brightly coloured lights flashed.

'Are you both ready?' Grandad asked.

The twins nodded, stepped forward and stood by the doorway that led into the time machine, which was juddering by now and making some strange and surprisingly ugly noises.

Grandad pulled a couple of levers, turned some dials, made some further adjustments on the screen and tapped several commands on his keyboard. The noises got even louder, and the machine began to whirr and shake so strongly that the ground trembled under their feet.

'Now!' Grandad shouted at the top of his voice.

As soon as they heard his command, Thomas

and Scarlett stepped through the doorway and into the darkness on the other side.

The workshop vanished, and so did Grandad, replaced by the blackness of space and the brightness of a million stars.

2

Scarlett saw a soldier on her right.

Another on her left.

More behind, more ahead.

Soldiers everywhere.

Each of them carried a spear in his right hand, a shield in his left, and a sword and a dagger strapped to his belt. Helmets protected

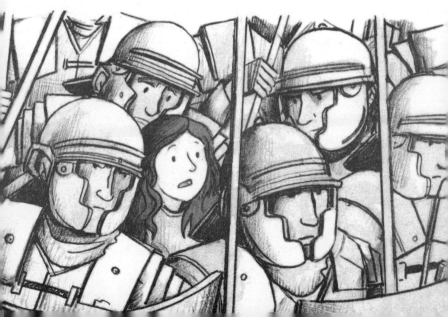

their heads, chain mail and armour covered their bodies, and they had sandals on their feet, giving them a good grip on the slippery grass.

They had been standing shoulder to shoulder, pressed together, but somehow a girl had appeared from nowhere and squeezed between them.

One of the soldiers started asking a question: 'What are you . . . ?'

Another asked at the same time: 'Where did you . . . ?'

Before either of them could finish their sentences, they were cut off by a loud voice.

'Silence! Face the front!'

The soldiers obeyed their centurion, ignoring the intruder who had suddenly come between them, and faced forwards, looking down the hillside at the enemy.

The time machine had deposited Scarlett into a line of Roman soldiers. She might have been only a kid, but she was hardly any shorter than many of them. She was, however, dressed very differently, wearing shorts and a T-shirt, whereas these men wore armour and carried weapons. In different circumstances, they might have laughed at Scarlett, or interrogated her, or even attacked her, but right now, preparing for battle, following the orders of their centurions, they barely even noticed her. All their attention was focused on the conflict ahead, and the enemy awaiting them.

'Steady the line,' came the voice from behind them. 'Wait for my word.'

The soldiers stood in silence. Disciplined and focused. Looking down the valley at the great mass of men and a few women who would soon be charging towards them. The two armies were surprisingly close together. Further than the length that a spear could be thrown, but that was all. Near enough that they could see

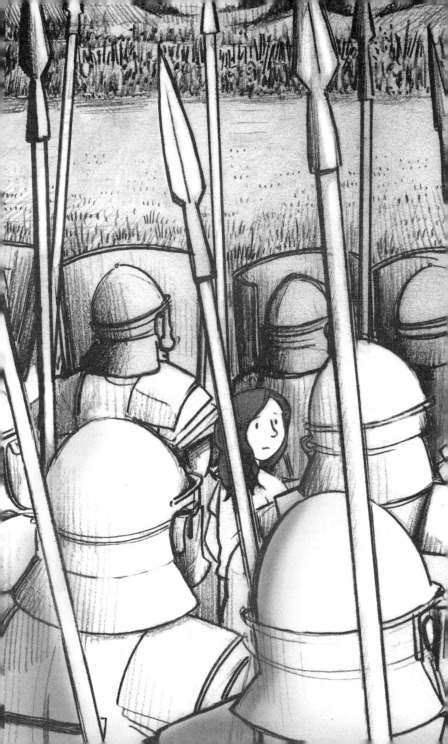

one another's faces.

'Keep your position,' came the voice again. 'For the glory of Rome. For the Emperor.'

The centurion was shouting in Latin, which Scarlett could understand, because her grandfather's device translated any words instantaneously.

She could also understand the men surrounding her, whispering to one another, a few in Latin, the others in different languages, speaking a mixture of tongues from all around the empire.

'They're a rabble,' someone said.

'We'll smash them to pieces,' agreed another.

'The hillside will run with their blood,' said a third confidently. 'They haven't got a hope. If they had any sense, they'd turn and run right now.'

Scarlett wondered if the men really believed what they were saying, or if they were speaking so bravely to hide their nervousness.

She could see a chariot at the front of the enemy. A driver stood at the front, a whip in his hand, ready to spur on the horses. Behind him, a woman stood at the back of the chariot. Scarlett couldn't see the woman's face, only her long red hair, flowing down her back.

The woman raised the spear clasped in her right hand, and yelled a command.

The noise died down.

The valley was quiet.

Nothing could be heard but the gentle twittering of a few birds. A buzzard mewed. The breeze shuffled leaves in the trees.

The woman started speaking. Her voice rang across the valley.

Was that Boudicca? Could it be her?

The warrior queen – that was what Miss Wellington had called her.

From this distance, Scarlett couldn't hear what the woman was saying, but she could see the effect of her words on the men and women surrounding her. They stood taller. They gripped their weapons and shields with more ferocity and determination. Their blood was hot, their spirits roused, ready for the battle ahead.

At the same time, Scarlett could feel the tension from the men around her. These soldiers might have been heavily armed, brilliantly trained, and almost certain of victory, but they couldn't help feeling a tremor of fear at what was awaiting them.

3

Thomas was lying on the wet grass. Above him was a wooden floor. No, not a floor, the base of a cart. He could see wheels on either side of him. Planks above him. Up ahead, the legs of two horses, which must have been tethered to the cart, ready to pull it away.

He rolled over and looked around.

In every direction, he could see legs.

Hundreds and hundreds of legs. Some bare, others clothed in woollen trousers. Many were barefoot, although others wore simple leather shoes or sandals.

If he wanted to see the rest of this huge crowd, and discover who they were, what they were doing, and where the wormhole had

deposited him, he'd have to crawl out of this space, and show himself.

He heard a voice.

Coming from directly above him.

A woman.

Shouting to be heard.

The translator in his ear allowed Thomas to understand every word.

'The Romans were proud,' the voice called out. Loud and clear and full of passionate intensity. 'The Romans were arrogant. The Romans thought they could conquer us.'

People booed and catcalled.

'The Romans thought we were weak,' the voice continued. 'The Romans were sure we would roll over and give up and do whatever they say. Were they right?'

Shouts around her: 'No! No! No!'

'The Romans thought they would never be beaten by a woman,' the voice went on. 'A mere woman! They laughed at us. They scorned us.

They said a woman could never lead an army against them. Were they right?'

More shouts. 'No! No! No!'

'We attacked them, and fought them, and beat them. My friends, we burned their towns to the ground. And now we shall drive every last one of them out of our land.'

A great cheer went up.

Thomas took advantage of the distraction to crawl out from under the end of the cart, skitter across the grass and stand up, joining the crowd.

Looking back, he realised that he hadn't been under a cart, but a chariot, drawn by two horses.

Around the chariot had been hung decorations. No, trophies. Ears, fingers, bones and skulls, presumably from warriors who had been slaughtered by whoever had ridden this chariot into battle.

On the back of the chariot stood a woman.

A tall, strong woman. With long red hair. Her face was painted with blue swirls, making her look wild and dangerous. She wore a magnificent long fur cloak over a grubby dress, which might once have been smart and beautiful, but was now smeared and splattered with blood and dirt. A spear was clasped in her right hand. She was the person giving the speech. The leader of this vast army.

Boudicca!

Surely this must be her.

She looked fierce, passionate, determined — and not scared of anyone or anything.

'This is our land!' Boudicca cried out to her army. 'We are a free people. We don't want to be ruled by Romans, or anyone else.'

From his vantage point, standing beside the chariot, Thomas looked around at Boudicca's army. Of course he could only see the nearest of them. He was in the middle of a vast crowd that stretched in every direction.

They all looked different. They had no uniform. A few had metal helmets and breastplates, many more had no armour to protect themselves and wore simple leather jerkins or even just smocks.

There were some warriors armed with spears, swords, axes or knives with sharp metal blades. Then there were archers with bows and arrows. Many had more basic weapons: Thomas saw axes made from a heavy stone tied to a stick; branches which had been sharpened to a point; and many men carrying nothing more than a stone clasped in their fist.

He spotted a few men wearing antlers on their head. Others had painted their faces like Boudicca, dyed their hair, or woven beads and

jewels into their beards. Some had strange tattoos on their arms and bodies. A group of musicians had drums hanging round their necks.

Thomas could see men of all ages – from old men with bald heads and grey beards to boys who must have been even younger than himself – but not many women. He wondered why. Where were the girls? Where were the rest of the women from these tribes? Hadn't they been inspired to join their leader in the battle?

'We gave the Romans a simple choice,' Boudicca shouted. 'Either they could leave our country, or they could die. They have chosen to stay – so let us drive them out of this life and into the next.'

When she said these words, a great cry went up. The drummers beat a wild rhythm. The men in antlers danced on the spot and chanted a wordless song. Many of the warriors shrieked and yelled, filling the air with a terrifying noise.

Boudicca let the noise continue for a few seconds, looking around the crowd as if she was drawing energy from their wild enthusiasm. She glanced at Thomas. When their eyes met, she seemed surprised. She looked at him for a long moment. Then she gave him a quick, encouraging smile.

Almost as if they knew one another.

Don't be silly, he told himself. Surely she gave the same smile to all her warriors, wishing them luck in the battle ahead. Filling them with strength and confidence.

Boudicca lifted her head, allowed herself one last look at her army, then turned round and issued an order to her driver. He flicked his whip and spurred the horses onwards.

The vast mass of people surged forward, cheering and shouting, whooping and hollering, charging up the hill, following the chariot –

and Thomas did too. He felt energised, even inspired, by the queen's smile. He might not be wearing any armour or be carrying a weapon, not even a stick or a stone, but he didn't care. He was going to fight by her side.

4

'Hold the line,' came the shouted command of the centurion, who must have been standing just behind Scarlett. 'For the glory of Rome. For the Emperor.'

Scarlett watched Boudicca's chariot juddering over the rough ground, coming up the hill, leading the charge. More chariots followed behind hers, and then the rest of the army, a vast mass of humanity. Thousands of them. Maybe tens of thousands. Weapons raised. Armour jangling. Drums beating. Voices crying out. Shouting and screaming and yelling. Rage and defiance and courage.

Up and down the line, the Roman centurions gave orders to their own troops. 'Hold your place. Don't break the line. Wait for my word.'

Scarlett waited with them.

She could see that the Romans were only a small group of men, vastly outnumbered by the army opposite.

And yet, looking at the forces facing one another, she thought the Roman soldiers were right to be confident.

They might have been facing a fierce opposition, a force much larger than their own little army, but they were better armed, probably better trained, and, most importantly, their commander had chosen a position for the battle which suited his own troops perfectly.

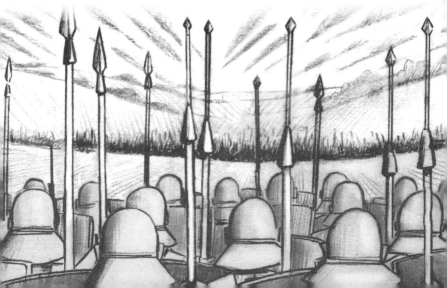

The Romans stood at the top of a steep hillside, looking down into the valley below.

The opposing army would have to struggle up here before engaging the Romans. They would be disadvantaged before they struck a blow.

As they came closer, Scarlett got a better look at the approaching army. They looked wild and terrifying. Some had painted their faces. Others were covered in tattoos. But very few of them had shields or helmets, let alone armour.

Some had spears or swords, but others looked as if they had simply grabbed the nearest implement – a spade, a scythe, a dagger, the axe that they had been using to chop some wood – before leaving their homes and joining the army.

The Roman centurion called out commands to his men. 'Hold the line,' he ordered them once again. 'Wait for my word.'

The soldiers did as they were told, and stood still, their spears raised, the points gleaming in the sunshine.

Here they came. Closer and closer. Faster and faster. The thunder of feet on the grass. The sound of a thousand voices screaming in rage. A great army charging up this hill. Following their leader, the wild red-haired woman on the chariot, her face painted bright blue, her mouth open in a defiant cry.

Scarlett gasped.

She couldn't believe it.

She had seen her brother! Thomas was in the midst of the crowd. Not far behind Boudicca's chariot. Running full pelt towards the Roman lines. Sprinting to keep up with the others.

Any moment now, he would

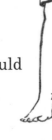

33

smack straight into a wall of shields. He had no weapon. No armour. Nothing to fight with. Nothing to protect himself against the sharp swords and spears of the Roman soldiers.

Turn round! Scarlett wanted to yell at him. *Get out of there! Save yourself!*

But she didn't say a word, because Thomas would never be able to hear her, and even if he had, how could he possibly fight against a tide of men and women, sprinting forwards, shouting, screaming, propelling themselves into the battle?

What else could Scarlett do? How could she save her brother?

A shout came from behind her. 'Javelins!'

The second line of soldiers – the men standing behind Scarlett – drew back their right arms, their javelins clasped in their fists.

'Ready!' came the command from their centurion.

The enemy thundered towards them.

The centurion yelled his order: 'Now!'

Together the entire line of soldiers hurled their javelins. A forest of spears flew through the air. The sky darkened for an instant. Then the javelins descended to the ground.

The noise was so terrible that Scarlett wanted to cover her ears. The sound of spearheads entering flesh. A multitude of voices screaming in pain.

But Boudicca's army didn't stop, didn't even pause. Anyone who fell to the ground was simply trampled under the feet of the men and women who came afterwards.

Scarlett heard a great clash of metal, followed by screams. The first soldiers had met in battle.

The noise increased. More and more

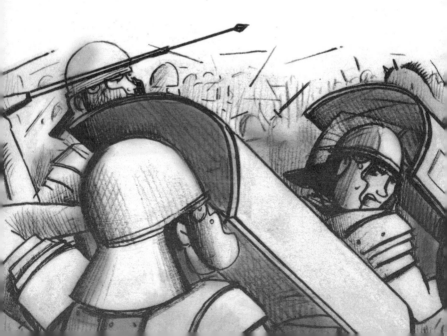

warriors joined the fight.

Here came Boudicca on her chariot, charging straight at the Roman lines. Her horses ploughed through the soldiers. She lunged at them with her spear.

An elbow hit Scarlett in the face.

She whirled round, then back, searching for her brother.

She caught a glimpse of his face in the melee of flashing steel and whirling bodies.

He was close enough that she could see the expression in his eyes. His fear. His panic.

He understood the peril. So why didn't he turn round and run back down the hill?

Because he couldn't.

There was no escape. Nowhere to run. For either of them. Thomas was being forced forward by the mass of bodies. Forced inexorably onto the line of Roman spears.

Suddenly he vanished.

One moment he was there, then he was gone.

Had he been trampled underfoot? Tripped and fallen? Or was there another explanation for his disappearance?

Scarlett reached into her pocket. No one would notice her disappearing from the battlefield. They were too busy fighting for their lives.

Hoping her brother had made the same decision, she pressed the button on her device.

5

Thomas ran up the hill, driven onwards by excitement and exhilaration, determined to stay close to his queen.

As the two armies came closer together, there was a sudden whooshing sound like the beating of a thousand wings, and a great darkness covered the sky. Then the javelins rained down on them.

Shrieks and cries rang out. Somehow he managed to avoid the spears, but he saw the damage all around him, the metal points thudding into flesh, men and women falling to the ground with a spear sticking out of them.

He had to keep running. Charging towards the opposition. No one could stop. Too many people were coming behind them. The army thundered onwards, screaming with fury, waving their weapons.

The Roman lines waited for them, cold and calm and unmoving, spears raised, shields up, an impenetrable wall.

Thomas could see what would happen next. He knew he had to get away if he wanted to survive.

He had no weapons. No armour. He wouldn't have a hope of leaving this battle alive.

Escape or die – those were his only options.

What about his sister? Where was she?

Maybe she wasn't even here? Maybe she had been sent somewhere else by the wormhole, a different place, even a different time?

If she was here, Scarlett would have to take care of herself. He couldn't help her. He had to save himself.

Thomas reached into his pocket. He was being jostled from every side, but he managed to pull out the device, put his finger on the button and press it down.

6

Scarlett and Thomas staggered out of the machine and into Grandad's workshop, where they found their grandfather standing in exactly the same place as before.

From his perspective, no more than an instant had passed between the moment that his grandchildren stepped through the doorway into the time machine and the moment that they came back again.

Quickly he clicked the main switch from ON to OFF.

The machine shuddered to a standstill. The lights stopped flashing, the strange noises faded into silence, and the workshop was quiet once more.

'How was that? Did the machine work?' Grandad reached for a pencil and a scrap of paper. 'I need to  know exactly what happened. What did you see inside the wormhole? What did you hear? What have you discovered about my time machine? Tell me everything.'

'We can tell you all about it later,' Thomas replied, still panting from the effort of running up the hill with the rest of Boudicca's army. 'Right now, we need to go back in time again.'

'Again?' Scarlett said. 'Why?'

'I want to know more about Boudicca. I want to meet her when she was younger.'

'It's too dangerous,' Scarlett said. 'We almost got killed!'

'But we didn't.'

'Mum and Dad are waiting for us.'

'Don't worry about that. No time passes in the present, remember?' Thomas turned to his grandfather. 'Grandad, we'll have to go back a few years earlier. Can we do that?'

'I don't see why not,' Grandad said. 'How far back?'

'Ten years,' Thomas said. 'Maybe twenty.'

'Sure.' Grandad span the dial. 'Sixty-one minus twenty is forty-one.'

'The Romans invaded in forty-three,' Scarlett said.

'Perfect.' Grandad nudged the dial two years forward, then flicked the lever from OFF to ON. Once again, the time machine shuddered into action. There was a loud groan, as if the mechanism itself was protesting. The noises started up again. Above them, the roof swayed backwards and forwards, the lights trembled, and even the walls started wobbling.

'I don't know if this is such a good idea,' Scarlett told her brother. 'Wouldn't it be better to go later? Shouldn't we wait till after lunch?'

'You can go later,' Thomas said.

'Why don't we talk about this first? Thomas? Thomas!'

Her brother ignored her, striding briskly towards the open doorway.

Scarlett darted after him. She grabbed his hand, and almost managed to hold on, but at the last moment her fingers slipped out of his. Together they tumbled into the darkness.

7

'Girl!'

The voice came from behind her.

'You, girl! Get up!'

Scarlett opened her eyes. She was sprawled on the ground. She could see dirt and grass and a pair of feet, encased in leather sandals.

Where was she? Where had the time machine brought her? And whose feet were those?

Hands grabbed her harshly. Fingers dug into her shoulders. Before she could resist, she felt herself being pulled up.

'Are you deaf?' came the voice again. 'I told you to get up!'

Standing upright, Scarlett found herself

face to face with a small, middle-aged woman in a brown smock. The owner of those nice sandals. She had blond hair, fair skin, blue eyes and an angry red face.

'Do you want to die?' she asked. 'Do you want the Romans to kill you?'

'No,' Scarlett said.

'Then get moving. You're a prisoner now, you have to behave yourself – if you want to stay alive.' The woman pointed. 'Go and stand in line with the others.'

Scarlett nodded and did as she was told, crossing the grass to join a line of girls. She saw that she had arrived in a campsite of some sort. Canvas tents had been erected in neat rows. She could hear barking dogs and someone practising the trumpet. Red flags fluttered in the breeze.

She stood at the end of the line. Some of the girls were about her own age, but most were a little older – teenagers, or perhaps even

in their early twenties. All were dressed in simple smocks, although a few had earrings, brooches, necklaces or other jewellery. They stared at her. Their expressions were curious and not unfriendly, but all of them looked nervous, as if they were worried about what might happen next. Scarlett wondered what they were doing here. Why had they come to this place? Why were they standing in a line? The woman had said she was a prisoner now. The Romans must have imprisoned them. But why?

The red-faced woman clapped her hands, demanding silence.

'The Emperor's daughter will be here in a moment,' she announced. 'You need to be on your best behaviour. No giggling, no jokes, no messing around. Bow your head to her. Do not say a word unless she asks you a question. Got that?'

The girls all promised that they had understood. Scarlett did the same.

'The Emperor's daughter will have a man with her who speaks her language and ours. Answer his questions carefully. Be quiet, be respectful, and perhaps you will be lucky enough to be picked as one of her slaves.'

A couple of the girls whispered to one another, until a harsh glance from the red-faced woman made them shut their mouths.

'You have all been taken from your families,' the woman continued. 'You're probably wondering if you'll ever see them again. The honest answer is: I don't know. Probably not. We're all slaves now. We're all prisoners. The Romans have taken over our country, but I can tell you this: I envy whoever gets chosen by the Emperor's daughter. She will have a much better life than the rest of us. If you've got to be a slave, it's much better to be the Emperor's daughter's slave than anyone else's.'

The woman made her way down the line, checking what each of the girls was wearing, adjusting their clothes and jewellery, brushing away any hair which had fallen out of place, and generally making them all look as attractive as possible.

When she came to the end of the line, she sighed.

'You could have made more of an effort,' she said to Scarlett.

'Sorry, miss.'

'Oh well, there's not much we can do now. Just try to smile, will you?'

'Yes, miss,' Scarlett said.

'And stand up straight.'

'Yes, miss.'

The red-faced woman was suddenly alert. She had spotted a small group of women walking towards them, accompanied by a man in a tunic and several uniformed soldiers.

She hissed a few final instructions to the girls. 'Remember, don't speak unless you're spoken to. Heads up. Smile. Look your best. Good luck, everyone.'

Some of the girls managed to do as they were told and stood taller, smiling, making themselves look good. Others were unable to conceal their fear and shrank back like frightened animals, terrified by the Romans approaching them.

8

Thomas was standing in the middle of a forest.

A moment ago, he had stepped through a doorway into the time machine, but there was no trace of his grandfather's workshop now, or his sister.

All he could see was trees.

Trees, trees and more trees.

He looked down and saw that he was standing on a path, a muddy track leading through the forest.

Which way should he go? This way? Or that way?

For no particular reason, he picked one direction rather than the other, but he hadn't taken more than a couple of steps when a voice shattered the silence.

'Stop!'

Thomas did as he was told. He looked around, trying to find the source of the voice, but there was no one to be seen. In fact, he could see nothing at all except trees – and he didn't believe that one of them would have shouted at him.

'Who's there?' Thomas asked.

No answer.

'Hello?'

Still no answer.

Maybe he had imagined the voice. His imagination must have conjured that shout out of the silence, inventing what he wanted to hear.

He started walking again, then stopped when some kind of projectile flew out of the trees and sped past his face, barely missing his nose.

What had that been? A bullet? An arrow?

It had passed so close to him that he'd felt its movement in the air. He looked around, searching for whoever had shot at him, but he couldn't see anyone.

Maybe he'd imagined that too. Maybe it had been an insect, not a missile.

He started walking again, but this time he only took one step before another missile flew through the air and thumped against his thigh.

'Ow!' he cried out. He clutched his leg with both hands and groaned in agony, scarcely able to believe how much it hurt. He'd have a big bruise later.

Down on the ground, he saw a stone, almost as big as a chicken's egg. If that had hit his head, rather than his leg, he would have been knocked unconscious.

Thomas looked around but he still couldn't see anyone. His attacker must have been hiding behind a tree. But which one? He wasn't

even sure which direction
the stone had come from.

What should he do?
Run? Or hide? But
where?

He put his hands
in the air.

'Hello? Whoever
you are, can you
stop throwing stones at me?
I really don't want to fight.
Come out and show me who
you are.'

He heard the crack of a branch.

He turned to look in that direction.

There was another noise behind him. He
spun round, but all he saw was trees, stretching
in every direction.

He heard a voice.

He whirled round.

Another branch cracked.

He heard a whistle.

He turned that way, but there was nothing to see.

He called out, 'Hello? Who's there?'

Suddenly he felt hands on his back, pushing him.

He turned, trying to see who had attacked him, and got a glimpse of a body, an arm. Then he was pushed from another direction. He stumbled forwards. A leg had been placed in his path. He tripped over and fell. Flat on his face.

He had a great weight on his back. Someone was sitting on him. He struggled frantically but couldn't escape. His arms were pinned down, his feet too. He couldn't even move. He was stuck. Trapped.

A prisoner.

9

The five women and the translator approached the line of girls. Scarlett had guessed immediately which of them was the Emperor's daughter. Dressed in a long, flowing white gown, she was the youngest of them, and could only have been twelve or thirteen, but she looked by far the most confident. She had a haughty, self-assured expression,

whereas the women surrounding her looked nervous and eager to please.

'Not her,' she said, dismissing the first girl with barely more than a quick glance. 'Look! Her ears stick out!'

The girl didn't know what the Emperor's daughter had actually said – unlike Scarlett, none of these girls could speak a word of Latin – but she understood that she hadn't been chosen and disappointment flooded her face.

The Emperor's daughter continued down the line, inspecting each of the girls, deciding whether any of them could be her personal slave.

'No,' she said. 'No, not her either.' She paused opposite a tall girl with angular features. 'This one is pretty, put her aside, she might do.'

That particular girl was told to step out of the line and wait, while the Emperor's daughter kept walking.

'Definitely not,' she said about the next girl in the line. 'I can't have a slave girl with wonky teeth. No. Maybe. No. No. Another maybe.'

Scarlett was sure that she was the only one of the girls who could understand what was being said, but she was careful not to show it, not wanting to draw attention to herself. She tried to replicate the expression that she saw on the others' faces: excited, yes, but also scared; unhappy to have been taken prisoner and worried about what might happen next.

The Emperor's daughter continued down the line. 'No. No. No. I like this one. What's your name?'

The translator posed this question, and the girl replied with her name.

'Cartimandua.'

The Emperor's daughter shook her head in disgust. 'What a very ugly name,' she said.

'You could change it for her,' the translator suggested.

'That's a good idea,' the Emperor's daughter agreed. 'We could give her a nice Latin name instead. She's a maybe, then. Keep her for now.'

Cartimandua was told to join the small group of maybes.

The Emperor's daughter kept moving down the line. 'No,' she said, ticking off each girl. 'No. No. No. Ooh, I like this.' She fingered an intricate bronze brooch that was pinned to the dress of one of the girls. It was in the shape of a hare.

'How beautiful,' the Emperor's daughter said. 'Can I have it?'

When the translator asked this question, the girl replied that yes, of course, the Emperor's daughter was welcome to take whatever she wanted.

'Thank you,' the Emperor's daughter said. She asked for that girl to be put aside, pinned the brooch to her own white tunic, then continued down the line.

'No. Maybe. No. No.'

When the Emperor's daughter reached the

end of the line, she stopped in front of Scarlett and took a long look at her face and her clothes, intrigued by what she was wearing.

'How strange these savages are,' she said, rubbing Scarlett's T-shirt between her fingers. 'I have never seen cloth like this. Isn't it ugly?'

Her servants nodded and agreed that, yes, those were the ugliest and most unpleasant clothes that they had ever seen.

The Emperor's daughter stroked the material, then gripped Scarlett's upper arm between her own thumb and forefinger and gave the flesh a strong pinch.

'Ow!' Scarlett yelped.

The Emperor's daughter took no notice. She pummelled and tweaked first that arm, then the other, testing Scarlett's muscles. She turned Scarlett's head from side to side, inspecting her profile, then motioned for Scarlett to open her mouth.

'I wouldn't want a slave with rotten teeth,' the Emperor's daughter said. 'Their breath smells awful.'

Scarlett didn't want to let anyone look inside her mouth, because they would spot the translator fixed to the back of her front teeth, so she said, 'You don't have to worry, I haven't got any cavities. My teeth are perfect.'

The Emperor's daughter stared at her in astonishment. 'You can speak Latin?'

'Only a little,' Scarlett admitted. 'I know a few words.'

'You're not Roman, are you?'

'No, my lady.'

'Then how do you know our language?'

'My father taught me to speak it,' Scarlett improvised. 'He was a merchant, trading with your people. He learned your language and taught me a few words.'

'He must have been a good teacher, you speak very well. What's your name?'

'Scarlett.'

'I like you, Scarlett. Let me smell your breath.'

Scarlett breathed out.

The Emperor's daughter sniffed, then nodded. She turned to the women accompanying her. 'I'll take this one. You can send the others away.'

The translator issued an order. The other girls shuffled away. One of them looked back sadly at her beautiful brooch. She knew she would never see it again.

'There's only one problem,' the Emperor's daughter said about Scarlett. 'Those ridiculous clothes. Lucia, take this girl away and put her in a decent tunic.'

'Yes, my lady.' One of the other women beckoned to Scarlett. 'Come here. This way. Follow me. We'll find you some proper clothes.'

10

Thomas was lying on the ground, pinned down, unable to move. His face was pressed into the damp earth. He could smell the leaves.

'Surrender?' said a voice.

'Yes, yes, I surrender.'

Whoever they were, they got off his back. Thomas rolled over, sat up, and saw that he was surrounded by a group of warriors.

No, wait a minute, they weren't warriors – they were kids. Most of them no older than himself and some quite a lot younger, certainly smaller. There were about twenty altogether. Boys and girls. Some carried stones in their fists, others were armed with sticks and a couple had knives.

He might have been able to fight one of them, or even two, but not all at once.

'Where did you come from?' one of the boys asked. 'How did you get past our guards?'

'It was like he appeared out of nowhere,' a girl said.

'How did you do that?' someone else asked him.

'I was walking through the forest,' Thomas said. 'You just didn't see me.'

He couldn't give any other explanation, and luckily the kids seemed to accept that one because they stopped questioning him about his sudden arrival in this place. Instead, they started discussing what to do with him.

'We could kill him,' suggested one of the boys.

'I'll do it,' said another.

'No, let me,' said a third.

The kids had fierce faces and crooked teeth. Most of them had long hair hanging round their shoulders. They wore ragged, dirty clothes and smelled like they hadn't had a bath for months.

Would they really kill him? They looked as if they might. How could he persuade them to let him go?

Slowly, taking great care not to make any sudden movements, Thomas hauled himself to his feet and turned around with his hands raised, letting them see that he didn't have any weapons and wasn't a threat to them.

'Let me go,' he said. 'I'll walk away. I won't tell anyone you're here.'

The kids discussed this amongst themselves. Some of them thought he should be freed, others recommended he should be tied up and kept as a prisoner, and someone suggested banging him over the head with a big stone.

One of the girls stepped forward. She had red hair and a fierce expression. She was about the same age and height as Thomas.

'What if he's a Roman spy?' she said. 'He'll run back to his friends in their army and tell them all about us.'

'He doesn't look like a Roman,' pointed out another kid.

The girl glared at him. 'How do you know what Romans look like?'

'I know better than you.'

'No, you don't.'

'Yes, I do, I've seen lots of Romans. They have dark skin and big noses.'

'His skin is darker than yours,' the girl pointed out. 'And his nose isn't that small.'

'The Romans aren't kids, they're soldiers.'

'There must be some Roman kids, otherwise they'd all die out.'

'Yeah, but they've been left behind in Rome with the women. They haven't come here. It's only men, only soldiers.'

The argument could have continued for hours but Thomas said, 'I'm not Roman. I promise.'

'That's exactly what you would say if you were a spy,' the girl pointed out.

'It's also what I would say if I wasn't a spy,' Thomas replied. 'Which I'm not.'

'He's right, Bou,' one of the other kids said. 'Let him go.'

Bou?

Thomas gave her a long look.

Could she be Boudicca? Really?

This small, skinny, grubby girl – could she

grow up into the warrior queen who had led a vast army into battle? She did have red hair, but she didn't look like the sort of person who would ever rule over a kingdom, let alone convince thousands of armed men to follow her to their deaths.

While he was staring at Bou, trying to work out who she might be, she was looking straight back at him, inspecting his features with the same intense interest. Perhaps she was checking the colour of his skin and the size of his nose. Eventually she must have decided that he wasn't a soldier and didn't pose any threat to herself and her friends because she nodded.

'Fine,' she said. 'You can keep walking. Get out of here. Go on, go, before I change my mind. We've got work to do.'

Having discovered who this girl was, or who she might be, anyway, Thomas didn't feel like going anywhere. He wanted to find out more about her.

'Work?' he said, trying to keep the conversation going. 'What kind of work are you doing?'

'It's none of your business,' the girl replied.

'Tell me. I'm interested. You're a bunch of kids, what important work could you possibly be doing?'

'Killing Romans,' the girl replied.

Thomas looked around. 'I can't see any.'

A couple of the kids laughed at this, but not Bou.

'Maybe we should kill you,' she said. 'You might not be Roman but you are quite annoying.'

'I've got a better idea,' Thomas said. 'I'll help you, let me join in.'

Bou sneered at him. 'You? How could you possibly help us? How many Romans have you killed?'

'None,' Thomas admitted.

'I thought not. Go on, get lost. Leave us alone.'

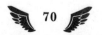 70

The other kids nodded, laughed and jeered.

'How about you?' Thomas demanded of Bou. 'How many Romans have you killed?'

'Twenty,' she replied.

'Twenty? Really?'

'Yes.'

Thomas stared at her. This girl who was armed with nothing more than a big stick, could she really have killed twenty Roman soldiers? She might have become a warrior queen in the future but could she really have been an assassin in the present?

Thomas shook his head. 'You haven't,' he said.

'Are you calling me a liar?' Bou squared up to him, ready for a fight.

'I'm just saying you haven't killed twenty Romans.'

'Admit it, Bou, he's right,' one of the others said with a laugh. 'You've never killed a Roman.'

'That's going to change,' Bou replied. 'Today.' She looked at Thomas. 'Do you want to kill your first Roman today too?'

Thomas didn't really want to kill anyone but he wasn't going to admit that. 'Yes, I do.'

'Then you can come with us.'

11

Lucia took a step back and looked Scarlett up and down, inspecting her own handiwork, then nodded.

'You'll do,' she said.

Scarlett was wearing a clean white tunic which Lucia had found for her. Her face had been washed, her hair pinned up and a simple leather necklace hung around her neck, strung with beads painted in many different colours. On her feet she was wearing leather sandals, each fastened with a long strap which had been wound round her ankles and tied with an elegant knot.

She wondered what would happen to her own clothes and how she could get them back again. She had asked exactly this question but Lucia simply told her not to worry, she would be given nice clothes by the Romans from now on, she didn't have to think about that old rubbish.

It's not rubbish! Scarlett wanted to say. *I really like that T-shirt, and Mum only bought me those shorts at the beginning of term, so they're practically brand new*, but she kept quiet, not wanting to invite any awkward questions.

She was given a small bag. Roman clothes didn't have pockets and an important person like the Emperor's daughter wouldn't carry their own belongings, instead handing them to a slave to hold for her. That was now Scarlett's job. She would have to follow her mistress wherever she went, carrying a bag which contained whatever she might need.

When Lucia's back was turned, Scarlett slipped the time-travelling device into this bag. If she got into trouble, she would press the button on the device and the wormhole would transport her back to the present, where her grandfather would be waiting.

'Let's go,' Lucia said. 'Come on, quick, she'll be wondering why we're taking so long.'

Lucia led Scarlett through the camp. The lines of tents seemed to go on for ever. The ground was uneven and muddy, having been trampled and turned over by a steady procession of feet, hooves and wheels.

The tents looked similar to some modern ones: they had four walls and a pitched roof, held up by poles inside the tent, and secured with taut ropes which were fastened into the soil with short wooden pegs.

Scarlett asked Lucia about the tents. 'What are they made from?'

'Goatskin,' Lucia replied.

'How many people sleep inside?'

'Usually eight soldiers,' Lucia replied. 'You'll share mine. There are already twelve of us inside so it's crowded. Our mistress has a tent to herself, of course.'

Through the open doorways of the different tents, Scarlett saw some men asleep, others cooking or eating, and yet more polishing their armour, sharpening their swords and spears, or bandaging their wounds. Strange sounds came from every direction: sawing and

hammering, ropes creaking in the wind, the roars of animals, men shouting orders.

Scarlett remembered a holiday with her parents and Thomas, a camping trip to Scotland. She'd hardly slept because of the wind battering the tent, her freezing cold sleeping bag, and the vicious midges who swarmed around them every evening and bit her all over, leaving her covered in red spots. It had been the worst holiday of her life! She felt sorry for these Romans having to sleep in a tent every night.

As they walked, Lucia gave Scarlett a few details about her duties, her responsibilities, and her new mistress, the Emperor's daughter.

'Her full name is Claudia Antonia, but she is always called Antonia. You will never call her that, of course. You will always call her "my lady". Do you understand?'

'Yes,' Scarlett said. 'Is she nice?'

'She'll treat you well if you work hard.'

That wasn't exactly an answer to her question, but Scarlett didn't insist on a better one.

'Are you a slave too?' Scarlett asked.

'Obviously,' Lucia said.

'So you're not Roman?'

'I'm not a citizen, no. I'm from Carthage. I was taken from there and brought to Rome and given to Antonia when she was only a baby.'

'How old were you?'

'Twelve,' Lucia answered. 'I'm now twenty-five, so I've spent more than half my life in

Rome, working for my mistress.'

'Don't you miss your family?'

'I can hardly even remember them,' Lucia said. 'Maybe I'll go back and see them one day. Antonia has promised that if I work hard for fifty years, she will free me. If you're lucky, she might do the same for you.'

12

The girl, Bou, led Thomas up the slope and into the shelter of the trees. Together they found a hiding place with a perfect view of the path below them.

The other kids had taken up their own hiding places too, all of them sheltered behind trees and bushes. Soon the forest was as quiet and peaceful as it had been, only moments earlier, when Thomas stood down there, dreaming away, never suspecting that he was being observed by a gang of twenty kids.

Thomas introduced himself. 'Your name is Bou, right?'

'That's what they call me,' the girl replied.

'Is that a nickname? Or your real name?'

'My real name is a bit of a mouthful.'

'What is it?'

'Boudicca.' She glared at him. 'Why are you looking at me like that?'

'No reason,' Thomas said.

The truth was, of course, that he had been remembering what she looked like in the future. A warrior queen addressing her army. Her face painted blue. Her long red hair cascading down her back. A fur cloak wrapped around her shoulders. A spear in her hand.

Her chariot hung with the skulls and bones of her enemies.

Do you want to know who you will become? he could have asked Bou. *Do you want to know who you are going to be twenty years from now?*

Should he try to persuade her to choose a different path? *Don't rebel against the Romans*, he could have warned his new friend. *And if you do, don't let them choose the place of your final battle, because they'll pick a battleground that suits them, not you.*

No, he couldn't say any of that. Even if he did, she wouldn't believe him. She'd think he was lying, telling silly stories, trying to pretend he could see the future.

Bou pulled a handful of slightly squashed strawberries from a pouch strung around her waist. 'Hungry?'

'Thanks.'

To Thomas's surprise, the strawberries were not only much smaller and harder than the fruits that he was used to, but tasted different too: they were sharp and tangy, rather than sweet.

'Where are the Romans?' he asked.

'They'll be here soon,' Bou replied.

She explained that lookouts had been posted further down the path in both directions. They were the youngest kids, the five- or six-year-olds, who wouldn't be much use in a fight but could keep watch for an approaching stranger and give a signal, warning the ambushers, telling them who was coming. One short whistle would mean a single traveller. A longer whistle signified a bigger group. A bird call would warn them that soldiers were coming.

'Who are you all? Where do you live? Round here?' Thomas asked.

Bou shook her head. 'We're from the north. We've come south to fight the Romans.'

'Do your parents know you're here?'

'My dad thinks I'm with my mum,' Bou said.

'And my mum thinks I'm with my dad.'

Thomas giggled. 'Is that the same for everyone here?'

'Pretty much,' Bou said. 'We didn't want to sit around at home, doing nothing, while the Romans were invading. We wanted to fight them. How about you? What are you doing in this forest? Do you live here?'

'Oh no, I'm from far away,' Thomas said.

'So you're not Catuvellauni?

Thomas didn't know what that meant, but he shook his head. 'No, I'm not.'

'You're not Iceni either, are you?'

'No.'

'Then how do you speak our language so well?'

Thomas came up with a lie. He pretended that his father was a merchant who traded with different tribes all over Britain and so the whole family could speak many different languages. Boudicca accepted his story. She must have known men like that, men who travelled up and down the country, and across the sea to Gaul or even Rome, buying and selling, negotiating and doing deals in many different languages.

Thomas asked her about the Romans. How long had they been in the country? When did they invade?

'A few weeks ago,' she replied.

'Why did they come here?'

'They're greedy. They want to steal our stuff for themselves rather than paying for it. We've been trading with them for years, since my grandfather's time and before. We buy their wine and their olive oil; they buy our tin and our slaves. But when Cunobelinos died, they thought they could have the whole country for themselves and steal our stuff without paying for it.'

'Who is Cuno . . . Cuno . . . whatever you said.'

'Cunobelinos was the king of the Catuvellauni,' Bou explained. 'When he died, he wanted to leave his kingdom to his eldest son, but his other sons bickered about it, and the whole kingdom fell to pieces. Now the Catuvellauni are fighting themselves, and all the other tribes are fighting too, no one can agree about anything. So the Romans were able to come ashore in their boats, march into the kingdom and take it over.'

Thomas was very interested by all this information. He couldn't wait to tell Scarlett. He knew how envious she would be that he had discovered the real reason that the Romans invaded Britain.

'So which of his sons do you think should be king? The oldest? The tallest? The nicest?'

'I don't care,' Bou replied. 'Cunobelinos wasn't my king, and his successor won't be either. We're not Catuvellauni, we're Iceni. We've come here with our own king,

Prasutagus.'

'Is he fighting the Romans too?'

'No, he's a wimp. He wants to make peace with them. He thinks we should surrender our weapons, give them our land and pay whatever tributes they want from us.'

'Shouldn't you do what he says? If he's your king.'

'He might be a king, but he doesn't understand what we really need to do to these Romans.'

'And what's that?' Thomas asked.

'Kill them,' Bou replied.

13

On the far side of the Roman camp, Lucia and Scarlett came to what looked like a building site. The shape of an enormous building had been mapped out with sticks and ropes, foundations had been dug in the soil, and rocks had been dumped in huge piles, twice the size of any man.

'What is this place?' Scarlett asked.

'It's nothing now,' Lucia explained. 'But it will be the temple when it's finished.'

'Which temple?'

'Ssh! No more questions. Don't speak unless you're spoken to. My lady doesn't like insolence.'

Lucia and Scarlett stood silently, side by side, waiting to be seen by their mistress.

Antonia was talking to a pale, slim, small man with narrow shoulders and thin arms. Although he was wearing a posh toga, he looked more like a scholar or a secretary than anyone important, and Scarlett assumed that he must work for the Roman army or government in some way. Perhaps he was in charge of organising travel arrangements for Antonia and her family. Or could he be an architect? Perhaps he had designed the new temple. He was holding a large sheet of parchment, covered with a detailed drawing, and he was pointing out details to Antonia, then gesturing at the field, explaining what would go where.

When Antonia eventually noticed her two slaves, she clapped her hands, delighted to see what Scarlett was now wearing. 'Oh, that's much better. You look very elegant. How lovely! Now I won't be ashamed to be seen with you.' She turned to the man beside her. 'This is my new slave. She's British, but she speaks perfect Latin. Come here, Scarlett. Say something for us.'

Scarlett didn't like the idea of performing for Antonia and this man, whoever he might be, but she didn't have much choice. She approached her mistress and the man in the toga and asked, 'What would you like me to say?'

Antonia grinned proudly. As if she had been the one who could speak two languages. 'You see, Daddy? Doesn't she have a good accent!'

'Very impressive,' the man said.

Daddy – so he must be the Emperor! Scarlett looked at the man with renewed interest.

He wasn't how she would have imagined an emperor; with his slim frame, and quick, nervous movements, he didn't look at all powerful or impressive.

He blinked short-sightedly back at her. 'What did you say your name was?'

'Scarlett.'

'And how did you learn to speak such excellent Latin?'

Scarlett repeated the story that she had given before, embellishing it with a few extra details, saying her father was a merchant who traded with Rome, and he had taught her to speak the language so she could help with his shipments and his accounts.

'Congratulations on finding her,' the Emperor said to his daughter. 'She'll be very useful as a translator if you ever want to speak to the locals.'

'Why would I want to do that?' Antonia asked. 'They're all savages, aren't they?'

'Yes, they are, but they're also part of the empire now. We have a responsibility to them. We must teach them how to live, how to behave. They might wish to visit Rome. Or fight alongside us. One day, their children, or their children's children, might even become citizens themselves.'

'I hope you won't let them,' Antonia said.

At that moment a young woman bustled into the room, followed by about a dozen slaves, some soldiers, and two children, a boy who must have been two or three, and a girl of four or five.

'Daddy! Daddy!' cried both children and rushed forwards to the Emperor, who swept them up into his arms.

'Leave your father alone,' the young woman said. She must have been about twenty years old, and was exceptionally beautiful. She held herself with the poise and confidence of someone who knows that she is the centre of

attention wherever she goes.

'Don't worry, Messalina,' the man said. 'I'm happy to see them.' He hugged both children. 'Hello, my darlings,' he said to them. 'What have you been doing today? What did you have for breakfast?'

'I had porridge with honey,' the little girl said.

'Was it nice?'

'Yummy.'

'Good. What about you, Tiberius? Did you have porridge too?'

'I hate porridge,' cried the little boy.

'So what did you have instead?'

'Pancake.'

'Delicious,' his father said. 'You're making me feel so hungry I might have to eat you up.' He pretended to take a bite out of his son.

The boy giggled excitedly, and cried out, 'No, Daddy! Don't eat me!'

'Oh, all right, not today, then.' He ushered the children towards Antonia. 'Go and say hello to your sister.'

She greeted them both formally rather than affectionately. 'Good morning, Tiberius. Good morning, Octavia. I hope you enjoyed a good night's sleep.'

'Aren't you going to say hello to me?' the beautiful woman asked.

'Good morning, Mother,' Antonia replied

with a smile which didn't have any warmth. 'I hope your night was very pleasant too.'

'It wasn't, it was horrible. I hate this place. I still can't understand why we had to come to this disgusting island. It's so cold! So grey! And the food is absolutely awful. I can't wait to get back to Rome.'

Scarlett couldn't work out the relationships between all these people. They appeared to be a family, but how did they fit together? The woman, Messalina, looked about twenty, and Antonia couldn't have been less than twelve or thirteen. How could they possibly be mother and daughter?

Obviously she didn't ask any of these questions. She hadn't forgotten that she was a slave who had no power here and could be thrown out at any moment. She stayed silent, keeping her eyes down and her expression serene, watching the scene without getting involved, playing the part of Antonia's faithful slave.

The Emperor asked his wife to be patient. 'You don't have to worry, my darling, we'll be heading home in a few days. We just have to accept an official surrender from the conquered kings, then we can all go back to Rome.'

'I can't wait,' Messalina said. 'Can we get on with it? Werc are these kings? Have they arrived yet?'

A soldier stepped forward to answer this question. He was a tall, broad-shouldered man, clad in a shiny breastplate and holding a helmet tucked under his arm. He had scars all over his face, and probably many more on his body too. He had big muscles, a deep voice, and looked as if he had never been scared of anything in his life. 'Emperor, the eleven kings are waiting for you now,' he said.

'Eleven?' the Emperor asked. 'I thought there were meant to be twelve.'

'The twelfth escaped,' the soldier replied.

'Escaped? How?'

'We lost sight of him after the battle. His name is Caratacus and he is one of the sons of Cunobelinos, the king of the Catuvellauni. He has neither an army nor any allies, so we'll track him down easily.'

'You'd better,' the Emperor said. 'I don't want any British kings leading rebellions against us, do you understand?'

'Yes, my lord,' the soldier said.

The Emperor asked for more details, demanding to know when these eleven had come to the camp, and how many soldiers each of them had been allowed to bring in their party. He wanted to know their names too, the names of their kingdoms, which of them was the most powerful, and any other useful information that the Roman spies had managed to gather.

Listening to their conversation, Scarlett learned that the Emperor, Antonia's father, was named Claudius, and the soldier was called Aulus Plautius.

Claudius ordered Aulus to inform the kings that he would be coming to meet them later.

Messalina clapped her hands at the two little children. 'Come on, Tiberius! Come on, Octavia! Who wants to ride an elephant?'

'Me, me!' they both cried.

'Good. Let's get you dressed up in your nice clothes. You're going to come and meet some kings.' Messalina turned to Antonia with an unfriendly smile. 'Are you coming too, darling?'

'Yes, Mother.'

'Then what are you doing, standing around dressed like that? Or do you want to make the savages feel at home by wearing clothes as ugly as theirs?'

'I'll go and get ready now, Mother,' Antonia said.

'You'd better be quick! You wouldn't want to be left behind, would you?'

'Yes, Mother. I mean, no, Mother. I'll go and get dressed right away, Mother.' Antonia gave a little bow first to Messalina, next to Claudius, then stalked away, her head held high.

Scarlett hurried after her mistress.

To pass the time while they waited for the Romans to arrive, Bou taught Thomas how to use a sling. She had a spare, which she let him borrow. It was nothing more than a piece of rope with a pouch in the middle to hold a stone.

Bou showed him how to fit a stone into the pouch, then swing the rope around and around, before finally letting the missile shoot out at great speed and enough force to kill a bird – or knock out a grown man if you managed to hit his forehead.

'You have to be careful to send it in the right direction,' she told him. 'My brother lost his two front teeth by hitting himself in the face with one of these.'

At first, Thomas was hopeless. He couldn't make the stone stay in the sling. He tried again and again, and each time the stone would drop straight out and fall on the ground. Once he finally managed to fit the stone in the sling and make it stay there, he found that he couldn't swing it properly. And even when he had mastered the basics, his aim was terrible. But slowly, repeating the same actions over and over, never giving up, he began to master the technique, and eventually even managed to hit the target that Bou chose: the trunk of a beech tree.

'Not bad,' Bou said. 'Now do it again.'

He tried again and missed, and then again and hit the tree.

'Good,' Bou said. 'And again.'

They continued practising, until Bou suddenly stood very still, her head cocked to one side, listening intently. Thomas could hear nothing except the sound of birdsong, which was what he had been hearing all day, but Bou knew better. She could distinguish between a real bird and one of her scouts whistling.

'They're coming,' she hissed. 'A group of soldiers.'

They threw themselves on the grass, peering down the slope at the path below.

Both of them were armed with slings, stones and a stick for close combat. Bou had sharpened the end of hers to a point.

Soon they heard a distant jangling as if someone was bashing pots together. The noise grew louder, then the first Romans appeared, coming round the bend in the path.

Two horsemen rode at the front of the column. Both were dressed in polished armour and plumed helmets. Behind them marched a column of soldiers, all dressed identically in red tunics with metal helmets and armour covering their shoulders and chests. Every one of them had a shield in one hand, a spear in the other, and a sword and a dagger hanging from his belt.

As they came closer, Thomas quickly counted the number of men. Thirty-two of them. Plus the two horsemen at the front of the line, and two more at the back. Thirty-six men. Heavily armed and armoured. Strong, fierce, battle-hardened. Against a bunch of kids who had nothing more than a few sticks and stones.

He glanced at Bou. Her face showed no trace of fear, only excitement at the fight ahead. He wished he felt the same confidence. How could she possibly defeat so many men? Surely it would have been more sensible to stay hidden, or even turn and run and hide in the woods, rather than challenge this small army?

Bou didn't even consider the thought of giving up. Once the column was level with their position, she leaped to her feet.

'Now!' she shouted at the top of her voice.

As soon as she gave the signal, stones rained down on the Roman soldiers. All the kids hurled the ammunition that they had gathered. Thomas joined in, swinging his sling and hurling a stone. To his disappointment, he saw it whistling over the soldiers' heads and disappearing into the undergrowth on the other side of the path.

Thomas could see the shock on the soldiers' faces. They put up their shields and sheltered from the onslaught. One man was hit in the face and doubled over, clutching his nose. Others cursed and shouted as stones smacked against their arms and legs, bouncing off their helmets, clanging against their shields and armour.

When the stones had been used up, Bou issued her next order. 'CHARGE!'

The kids ran down the slope towards the road, waving their sticks in the air, and threw themselves at the soldiers.

Bou ran faster than anyone and joined the battle first.

Thomas found himself caught up in the excitement. Shouting at the top of his voice, he sprinted down the slope, and swung his stick at the nearest soldier.

The man raised his shield.

Thomas's stick smacked against it – and broke in half.

Thomas stared stupidly at what was left of his weapon. Then he looked up – and saw a fist coming towards him. He managed to dodge away, but the punch still connected with the side of his head. He was stunned. Dizzy. Confused. And didn't even notice the next punch coming, the one that knocked him to the ground.

15

Antonia strode through the camp to her own tent. Scarlett practically had to jog to keep up. Soldiers leaped out of their way. Antonia didn't stop once. Didn't even pause. She stared straight ahead, her eyes fierce, her expression proud and determined.

Once they were in the safety of the tent, Antonia closed the flaps, shielding them from view, and let her real feelings out. She raged and stormed, kicking over a chair, then picking up a plate and hurling it to the ground.

'I hate her,' she hissed to herself. 'I hate her. I hate her. I hate her.'

'Your mother?' Scarlett asked.

'My what?' Antonia turned on her with

rage in her eyes.

'That woman with the Emperor,' Scarlett managed to say. 'Isn't she your mother?'

Antonia gave a scornful laugh. 'My mother is a wonderful woman. Kind, loving, clever and utterly devoted to me. She was devoted to her husband too, until he decided to divorce her. She is the opposite of that woman in every way.'

That woman – she made the words sound like an insult.

'She looks a little younger than him,' Scarlett said.

'A little?' Antonia laughed. 'She is twenty-one and he is fifty-three.'

'Those children – they're your half-brother and your half-sister?'

'Exactly.'

Antonia explained the relationships between the different people in her complicated family and how they fitted together. Her father,

Claudius, had never expected to become the Emperor, she said. He was a writer, not a politician or a soldier. He had written a long series of history books, an autobiography, and a book about his love of playing dice. No one ever thought he would do anything else with his life, let alone become powerful or important. But to his own surprise, and everyone else's, he had been made Emperor after the death of Caligula, only two years previously.

'His first wife gave him a son, who died as a baby. His second wife was my mother. His third wife, Messalina, has provided two children, a girl, Octavia, and a boy, Tiberius. If he's lucky, and doesn't get murdered first, Tiberius will be the Emperor one day.'

'Who would want to murder him?'

'Who wouldn't?'

Saying those words, Antonia gave a careless laugh, which surprised Scarlett. What was so funny about murdering someone? Particularly if that person was a little boy, who can't really have hurt anyone in his life, however horrible his mother might have been.

Perhaps Antonia guessed what Scarlett was thinking, because she gave her a rueful smile. 'Don't worry,' she said. 'I'm not going to kill him myself. Even if I want to sometimes.'

'Brothers can be very annoying,' Scarlett agreed.

'You have a brother?'

'Yes.'

'How old is he?'

'Twenty minutes younger than me. We're twins.'

'I'd like to meet him. Where is he now?'

'I have absolutely no idea,' Scarlett answered.

Suddenly Antonia remembered why she had returned to her tent. She needed to get dressed for the ceremony. She called out, 'Lucia? Where are you, Lucia?'

There was no answer.

'Where is Lucia?' Antonia said. 'I need to get ready.'

'Why don't you skip the ceremony? If you don't want to go.'

'That would only make Messalina even happier.' Antonia opened the tent's flaps and called out, 'Lucia! Where are you, Lucia? Come here! I need you!' She listened for a moment, but there was no response. She turned to Scarlett. 'Go and find Lucia, will you? Tell her I need to get dressed.'

'Where is she?' Scarlett asked.

'She's probably washing clothes. You'll find her by the river.' Without another word, Antonia turned her back on Scarlett.

'Where's the river?' Scarlett asked, but Antonia took no notice. Scarlett understood that she would have to find it herself. She left the tent and walked through the camp, asking for directions from various soldiers.

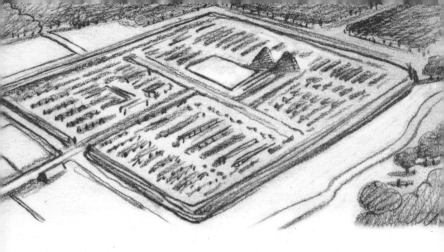

The camp was surprisingly large. The neat rows of tents seemed to go on for ever. High wooden walls marked the camp's boundary. Guards watched the surrounding landscape from tall platforms.

Soon Scarlett came to a gate in the walls. Six men stood by the gate, checking who came in and out. They interrogated Scarlett briefly, asking her name, and the name of her master.

'Claudia Antonia is my mistress,' she replied.

Hearing the name of the Emperor's daughter, the guards immediately let her past. One of them pointed the way to the river.

Scarlett jogged down the hillside and found Lucia kneeling on the riverbank, laying out wet clothes on the grass.

'Lucia,' Scarlett called out. 'Antonia wants to see you.'

'Help me with this.'

Together Lucia and Scarlett pulled the sodden clothes from the river, squeezed out most of the water, and laid them to dry on the grass, then hurried back to the camp.

16

The Roman soldiers made the kids stand in a line.

The battle had been short and swift. A bunch of kids armed with sticks against a heavily-armed, highly-trained column of soldiers – there was only ever going to be one victor.

A few of the Romans had been wounded. Some of them were clutching their heads, legs, or arms, rubbing their wounds. One of them

had blood running down his face. But all of them were still on their feet.

Bou had been wrong. Today wasn't the day that she was going to kill her first Roman.

She and the others might have been captured, but they still looked defiant. If they were scared, they didn't show it. Thomas tried to do the same.

He remembered what Bou had said about Romans: they had dark skin and big noses. That was certainly true of some of these soldiers, but not all of them. Some were dark-skinned, others pale. They had noses of different shapes and sizes. He had expected that they would all look Italian, but in fact they looked as if they came from lots of different parts of the world.

The Roman commander paced up and down, inspecting his prisoners and discussing the next move with his second-in-command.

With Grandad's invention in his ear, Thomas could eavesdrop on their conversation.

He quickly discovered that the commander's name was Longinus.

To his horror, he heard the Roman centurions discussing only two possibilities for their prisoners. Either they would take the children back to the camp and sell them as slaves. Or they would slaughter them right here.

They're kids, Thomas wanted to shout out. *They're only kids! Sure, they might have wanted to kill you, but they didn't, did they? How much damage did they actually do? A few bruises, nothing more. You can't kill them or sell them as slaves. That's disgusting. You should let them go.*

Perhaps he should have revealed that he could speak their language and told them what he was thinking. Instead, he kept quiet and listened to their discussion, and heard them agreeing that they would keep the children, take them back to the main camp and arrange for them to be sold as slaves.

He would conceal his knowledge of their language for a little longer, he decided. With any luck, he would be able to pick up some valuable information which he could use to escape, freeing Bou and the rest of her friends at the same time.

The kids were quickly tied up. The Romans had a simple method of securing their prisoners, clipping a metal loop around their necks, then slotting a rope through every loop, so none of them could run away without dragging the rest of the prisoners with them. They had already confiscated any sticks, knives or catapults, and now patted the children down, searching for hidden weapons.

One of the soldiers found the device in Thomas's pocket. He called one of his colleagues over. 'Look at this,' he said. 'What do you think it is?'

It's a device for travelling through time, Thomas could have said. *Press that button and you'll be sucked into a wormhole.*

Obviously he didn't say that. He didn't want the soldier to disappear from this time and arrive in Grandad's workshop. That wouldn't be good for Grandad, who would have to defend himself against an armed soldier. It wouldn't be much good for the soldier either, who would almost certainly end up in prison or hospital. 'This man thinks he is a Roman soldier,' the doctors would say, while scratching their heads. 'The strange thing is, he speaks perfect Latin.'

Not wanting to give away the fact that he could speak their language, Thomas didn't say a word himself but held out his hand, begging to be given back his property.

The two soldiers ignored him, and instead took turns to inspect the device. 'It's so shiny,' one of them said.

'Look at this,' replied the other, tapping the screen. 'Do you see?'

'What's going on there?' The shout came from one of the centurions. 'Why are you taking so long?'

'Confiscating weapons, sir,' the soldier called back.

'Get on with it! We need to move on.'

'Yes, sir.'

The soldier dropped Thomas's device on the grass, and stamped on it with his heel. 'Come on. Get in line,' he snarled.

Thomas stared in horror at the smashed device. How was he ever going to get home again? Somehow he'd have to find his sister – or he'd be trapped here for the rest of his life.

The soldier shoved him. 'Didn't I tell you to get in line?'

17

'I don't like that one,' Antonia said. 'Try this one instead.'

Scarlett handed the silk stola back to Lucia, picked another from the wooden pole hanging at the back of the tent and held it over herself, showing how it would look. There weren't any mirrors in the tent, so Antonia had to make a decision by viewing each of stolas on one of her slaves. Antonia was already wearing a tunic not very different from the ones worn by Scarlett and Lucia, although theirs weren't as neatly-cut or luxurious as hers. Over the top of the tunic, she would wear a stola, a long sleeveless dress, fastened with two belts. She had six to choose from, each differently coloured, some plain, others decorated with beautiful embroidery. Two were silk, the others woven from fine wool.

Scarlett and Lucia were helping Antonia get ready for the big ceremony that would be happening later that day. She had already bathed, washing herself in buckets of warm water which other slaves had brought to the tent, then covered herself in sweet-smelling perfume.

Antonia narrowed the choice down to two.

'You decide,' she ordered Scarlett. 'Which of them would look better on me?'

'This one, my lady.'

Antonia considered the stola for a moment, then nodded. 'Good choice. I'll wear it.'

'You might want something warmer,' Lucia said to her mistress. 'Like that one, for instance. The weather on this island is so horrible. Do you think the sun ever shines here?'

'Probably not,' Antonia replied. 'That's why the natives look so depressed all the time.'

'What's wrong with staying in Rome?' Lucia asked. 'We have everything there. Nice weather. Good food. Why does he want to come to the end of the world? What if we fall off?'

Antonia laughed. 'You're not going to fall off the edge of the world, you silly woman. It's round.'

Lucia was amazed. 'Round? Really? How do you know?'

'Everyone knows that,' Antonia replied.

'I didn't,' Lucia said. 'I thought it was flat.'

'That's because you're an idiot.' Antonia looked at Scarlett. 'What do you think? Is the world round or flat?'

Scarlett wasn't sure how to reply. She didn't

want to give any hint that she came from a different time or possessed more knowledge than she should have had if she was an ordinary local girl. But what did people really think two thousand years ago? If she'd lived in these times, how much would she have known about the shape of the planet? In the end, she decided to copy Lucia.

'I've always thought it was flat,' Scarlett said.

Antonia burst out laughing. 'Another idiot! I'm surrounded by them.'

Scarlett said, 'How do you know the world is round?'

'Ask anyone in Rome and they'll say the same. Anyone with half a brain, anyway.'

'But how do you know?'

'Some philosopher worked out the reason. I can't remember how he did it. Something to do with a tower and a shadow. I don't know. Does it really matter?' She pointed at the tunic that

Scarlett had suggested. 'Come on, help me get dressed.'

While Antonia was being fitted into her stola, she and Lucia chattered about the events of the day ahead, and what had been happening recently. Scarlett managed to pick up a few useful snippets of information. She already knew that both Lucia and herself were the slaves of Claudia Antonia, the daughter of the leader of all Romans, Emperor Claudius. He and his family had arrived in Britain to celebrate his triumph over the local tribes.

The actual battles had been won by Aulus Plautius, who had already been in Britain for a few months. He had come with an army and fought several battles against the local tribes. When they surrendered, Claudius had come from Rome to take credit for this military success.

Therefore she must be in the year 43. She had been reading about the Roman invasions of Britain. Julius Caesar had brought an army here in 55 BC, then again in 54 BC, but he hadn't stayed for longer than a few weeks. Almost a hundred years later, Claudius had tried again, this time defeating the Britons and making this island into a part of the empire.

She would have liked to ask if they were definitely in the year 43 but she couldn't ask what year it was. Antonia wouldn't have been able to answer her question, or not in any way that Scarlett would have understood.

The Romans had their own method for counting years, and they certainly wouldn't have thought of the calendar beginning in the year that Jesus Christ was born. Antonia and Lucia almost certainly wouldn't even have heard of Jesus. If by any chance they had, they would have thought that he was a minor Jewish prophet who had managed to offend almost everyone during his short and unsuccessful life, and would have been astonished to discover that his name was still remembered two thousand years in the future.

Scarlett wished she knew more about Emperor Claudius, but although she had been reading about the Romans that morning and learning about their various conquests, including their invasions of Britain, she couldn't remember anything about the emperor who had brought his armies here.

'Give me those pins,' Antonia ordered Scarlett.

'Yes, my lady,' she replied, and hurried to fetch a selection of beautiful hairpins which had been set out on a low table. Some had been carved from ivory or stone, others made from bronze or silver. She offered the selection to Antonia, who picked the ones that she wanted, and Lucia used them to pin up her hair.

Antonia let out a shriek. 'Ow! Idiot! You stuck that pin in my head.'

'Sorry, my lady,' Lucia said. 'I'm so sorry.'

Antonia had been moving around so much that Lucia couldn't help hurting her, but she took the blame herself, apologising several times, and promising not to do anything so silly ever again.

'You'd better not,' Antonia said. 'Or you'll spend the rest of your life working in a salt mine, not enjoying a cushy life as my slave. You don't know how lucky you are.'

'Oh, I do, my lady. I thank the gods every day for my good fortune.'

'You shouldn't just thank the gods,' Antonia said. 'You should thank me too.'

'I do, my lady. I thank you for your goodness and your kindness. You are the best mistress that any slave could hope for.'

'I am,' Antonia said with a self-satisfied smile. 'Now, come on, stop talking so much, you silly girls. Help me with this. You remember what my father said, I have to look my best for all these savages. We want them to see all the

grandeur of Rome and understand why they'll
be happier as part of the empire.'

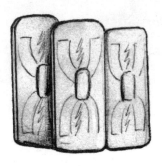

The column of Roman soldiers and the line of British prisoners marched for a long time through the woods. At first, the soldiers insisted that no one spoke, but they soon forgot to insist on silence, and the children chatted as they walked, encouraging one another and even singing songs to keep their spirits up.

They passed through a village. Barking dogs ran out to scare them off, then backed away when one of the soldiers thrust his spear in their direction. The houses were round and timber-framed with conical thatched roofs. The locals stayed inside, peering nervously through the doors at the soldiers and their prisoners.

Bou sniffed the air. 'Cabbage soup. Yum. That's exactly what I'd like right now.'

Unfortunately, they didn't get a chance to sample any of the local cuisine, because the Roman soldiers hurried them onwards, down a rough track which led away from the village and back into the forest.

They walked for a long time. Several kids muttered complaints, but the soldiers took no notice, not allowing anyone to stop for a rest, let alone get a drink or have anything to eat.

Just as Thomas was beginning to worry that he might collapse from hunger, thirst and exhaustion, Bou pointed out their destination, a town on a hilltop.

'That is Camulodunum,' she told Thomas. 'You remember I told you about Cunobelinos? The king of the Catuvellauni.'

'The one who died? Whose sons have been fighting one another?'

'Exactly. This is his city, his capital. The Romans defeated the Catuvellauni army and took this place for themselves.'

Camulodunum – Thomas had never heard of anywhere with that name. He wondered if the town still existed, and if so, what it might be called in his time.

They crossed a river, passing a line of small boats which were unloading supplies, and marched up the hill. Thomas saw shattered armour and broken weapons left on the grass, which must have been discarded during a brutal battle not long ago.

The Romans had burned much of the town

to the ground. Previously Camulodunum had been a settlement of round houses like the ones that Thomas had seen earlier in the village that they had passed through. Now, most of those houses were blackened ruins, their roofs collapsed. A few small children ran through the debris. Dogs sniffed, searching for scraps, and sheep and goats nuzzled the grass.

Having destroyed Camulodunum, the Romans had replaced the town with their own camp, which they had built at the top of the hill. From the scale and precision of their work, it looked as if they intended to stay for a long time. They had dug a deep ditch around the perimeter of the camp, then built high wooden walls, topped with sharp stakes. On each corner of the camp, guards stood on raised platforms which gave them an excellent view of the surrounding countryside. If any native forces tried to attack the invaders and take their territory back, they would have to climb the hill and cross the ditch, then climb the wall before engaging in hand-to-hand combat with the Roman soldiers.

The entrance gate was guarded by several soldiers, who interrogated the centurions, asking their names, before standing aside to let the convoy pass.

The camp was buzzing with energy and activity. Men were putting up tents, practising their fighting skills, organising food stores, exercising the horses and carrying great bundles of armour and weapons. Groups of soldiers marched past. A couple of cooks carried big pots. Men led sheep and goats through the camp, presumably taking them to be milked or slaughtered to provide food for all the soldiers.

Thomas remembered a holiday with his

parents and Scarlett, a camping trip to Scotland, where they had climbed mountains, swum in a cold loch and camped in a huge field, cooking their meals over a little stove. It had been brilliant! He felt envious of these Roman soldiers, getting to sleep in a tent every night.

Still tethered together with a rope attached to the metal hoops around their necks, the kids were led to a part of the camp where prisoners were kept, awaiting their fate. There must have been a couple of hundred people there, mostly men, along with a few women. Everyone stared curiously at the line of children, wondering why they should have been captured and brought here.

Thomas, Bou and the other kids were left for a long time, guarded by a couple of bored soldiers. At first, these two soldiers stopped any conversation, slapping or kicking anyone who dared to speak, but they soon lost interest in policing the children, instead chatting to a few of their comrades who were guarding other prisoners.

'I'm starving,' Bou said.

'Me too,' Thomas agreed.

'If you could eat anything right now,' Bou said, 'anything at all, what would you eat?'

'Sausages and mash,' Thomas replied without a moment's hesitation.

'Sausages? Mash?' Bou didn't know the words. 'What are they?'

Thomas remembered that potatoes hadn't arrived in Britain yet, and wouldn't get here for another fifteen hundred years. And didn't they have sausages? He felt sorry for them. 'Meat and vegetables,' he said. 'Followed by more of those strawberries. They were delicious. What about you?'

'My mum's nettle soup,' Bou replied. 'With fresh bread, two boiled eggs, and some blackberries with honey.' Suddenly she clutched her stomach. 'Oh no, let's talk about something else, this is making me too hungry. What shall we talk about instead?'

'How we're going to get out of here,' Thomas suggested.

'I wish I knew,' Bou replied.

Merchants wandered among the prisoners, looking for good specimens. These merchants followed the Roman army, both in this country and others, buying loot from the soldiers, selling them food, drink or souvenirs. Some of the merchants specialised in slaves, and hoped to buy prisoners from the army – men, women, or children who had been captured in battles and would be sold off quickly, then could be transported to another country and sold again at a good profit.

A couple of merchants were already negotiating with one of the soldiers, trying to buy some burly British warriors, hoping to take them down to the river and put them to work in a boat, pulling the oars.

Some of the merchants came to have a look at the children.

'There's only one problem with buying kids,' one of them said. 'You never know what you're getting. They might grow up strong or they might be weak. They might be good workers, but they might be lazy, you just don't know. That's why I never buy anyone under fifteen. I'd rather spend my money on the finished article.'

'That's why they're cheap,' said another man. 'You're taking a risk. You might get a good one, you might not. Personally I think it's a risk worth taking.'

Thomas felt furious. He hated hearing these merchants talk about himself, Bou and the rest of the kids as if they were animals or objects rather than human beings. He was desperate to get away. Somehow he had to escape, and take the others with him. But how?

Some of the merchants spoke the same language as Bou and the other kids. She argued with them.

'You shouldn't work with the Romans,' she said. 'You should be fighting them, not trading with them. Don't you even know the difference between right and wrong?'

'Sorry, miss,' answered one of the merchants. 'I need money to feed my family. I can't care about right and wrong.'

'Doing the right thing is more important than earning money,' Bou insisted.

'Not when you're got a house full of hungry kids,' the merchant replied. 'Listen, I can understand why you're upset. No one wants to be a slave. But the Romans are good bosses. If you work hard and behave yourself, after twenty or thirty years they might even give you your freedom.'

Thomas was shocked. 'Thirty years? Are you serious?'

'It's better than being a slave for your whole life,' the merchant said.

He was about to continue walking around the camp, inspecting the rest of the prisoners, looking for some nice strong slaves to buy and sell as farm workers, when Bou called him back.

'Will you buy us and set us free?' she asked him.

The merchant laughed. 'Why would I want to do that?'

'You're not a Roman, are you?'

'No.'

'Where are you from?'

'Venta,' he replied.

'We're Iceni,' Bou told him. 'We're allies, your people and my people. You should help us. Buy us, set us free and together we'll attack these Romans, and get them out of our country.'

Hearing her words, the merchant looked around nervously, checking that none of the soldiers had overheard what was being said.

Bou laughed at him. 'You don't have to

worry,' she said. 'They can't even speak our language.'

The merchant hissed at her. 'Let me give you a piece of advice, young lady,' he whispered. 'Keep quiet, behave nicely and do what you're told. It's your only chance. These soldiers don't mess around. They'll kill you simply for answering back.'

'Who cares?' Bou replied. 'They can get lost. I don't want them in my country.'

'It's their country now.'

'Traitor! Untie these ropes. Let me go.'

'Not a chance.'

'You'd better. Or you're going to be in big trouble.'

The merchant laughed. 'Oh yeah? What are you going to do to me, little girl?'

Bou fixed him with a fierce glare. 'I'm going to escape from these stupid Romans,' she said. 'And when I get out of here, I will find you and I will punish you.'

The smile faded from the merchant's face. She might have been a girl; she might have been smaller than him, and much younger; she might have been tied up with rope and a metal collar, but her fierceness and determination still managed to scare him. Muttering to himself, he hurried away, stopping only to give a quick glance over his shoulder at Bou, as if he was making sure that she hadn't somehow managed to follow him.

19

A soldier came to collect the Emperor's daughter from her tent. He introduced himself to Antonia, announcing his name and rank: 'Marcus Favonius Facilis, centurion, at your service, my lady. Your father asks for your presence. The ceremony is about to begin.'

'Yes, yes, I'm ready. No need to hurry me along.'

Antonia might only have been thirteen years old, and living in the year 43, but she looked as glamorous as any twenty-first-century model or movie star. She was wearing the perfectly embroidered silk stola over her tunic, and a woollen shawl, a palla, to keep her warm in the miserable British weather.

She was wearing her hair up, held in place with ivory pins, and she had been adorned with beautiful jewellery: intricate gold anklets and bracelets, long silver earrings dripping with diamonds, and a thick gold necklace, which weighed as much as a bag of flour, and must have been hard work to wear around her neck.

Lucia and Scarlett were both still wearing their own ordinary simple tunics. Neither of them had any jewellery or perfume.

They followed their mistress out of the tent. When they emerged into the daylight, they discovered that Marcus had brought six guards with him, an escort to accompany the Emperor's daughter through the camp.

'This way, my lady.' Marcus and his soldiers were about to lead Antonia away, but she refused to move.

'What about my slaves?' she said. 'I want to bring them too.'

'That won't be possible, my lady. Your father has ordered that you will be riding one of the elephants, and there isn't room for three.'

'Is there room for two?'

'There should be, yes, my lady.'

'So I can take one of them?'

'I suppose you can, my lady.'

'You can come with me.' Antonia snapped her fingers at Scarlett. 'Come on, don't hang around, let's go. We don't want to keep Daddy waiting. Lucia, you can finish the laundry.'

Lucia looked unhappy about that. Scarlett could understand why. Given the choice between doing laundry and riding an elephant, she wouldn't have chosen to wash tunics in the river either.

The soldiers escorted Antonia and Scarlett, Marcus and three of his men walking ahead, clearing a path through the crowd, then three more walking behind, making sure no one came close to the Emperor's daughter.

Scarlett was surprised to see so many locals milling around. The camp was full of people, not just soldiers, but hundreds more people. Some must have come from nearby towns and villages, while others might have followed the army across the country, and perhaps even

across the continent. As she and Antonia walked down the lines of tents and along the muddy tracks, they passed beggars with outstretched hands, and merchants offering bread, fruit or meat for sale. Some women stood in a group, chatting to the soldiers. People turned and gawped at Antonia. Probably none of them knew who she might be, but they must have been able to tell that she was wealthy and important, and so they wanted to have a good look.

20

Thomas felt as if he'd been standing in that field for hours. His legs ached. He wished he'd never travelled back in time. He could have been at home, eating some delicious lasagne rather than hanging around here, roped and chained, waiting to be sold, imprisoned or murdered.

Lasagne! The very thought of his mum's cooking made him feel even worse. He tried to put it out of his mind, but somehow that made him feel even hungrier and thirstier. The thought of home made him think about Scarlett too, and he wondered where she might be and what had happened to her. It was his fault that they'd come back to this time. She'd wanted to take her time, have lunch first and think things through. Yes, she'd been right, he didn't mind admitting that. He hoped she was safe and her situation was better than his.

He and the other children hadn't been given anything to eat or drink. They weren't even allowed to use a toilet. If anyone needed to go, they simply had to walk as far away as the rope would allow them, and squat in the mud. Soon the whole place started to stink.

Merchants had been walking around all day, inspecting the prisoners, but luckily none of them wanted to buy any children. Thomas had seen other prisoners being taken away, the merchants handing over handfuls of silver and bronze coins to the Roman guards in exchange.

He heard a bizarre noise, almost like a trumpet, which reminded him of a nature documentary. When the noise was repeated, he realised where he had heard it before.

'That sounds like an elephant,' he said.

'An elly-what?' Bou asked.

'It's a big animal with a long trunk. A long nose. Like this.' Thomas acted out an elephant.

Bou burst out laughing. 'Don't be silly. That's not real! There aren't any animals like that. Only in stories.'

'You don't have to believe me,' Thomas said. 'But elephants are totally real.'

Bou just laughed even louder, then jumped to her feet and imitated Thomas, pretending to be an elephant herself.

Longinus came hurrying down the line, bringing more of his troops. Since Thomas had last seen them, the men had been polishing their weapons and armour, smartening themselves. Perhaps they were going to be inspected or take part in some kind of ceremony.

The two guards snapped to attention.

Longinus issued an order to them. 'It's time to go,' he said. 'The Emperor wants these prisoners to be present at the ceremony. To show the British what will happen to anyone who dares defy the Roman army. Let's go. Come on.'

The guards yanked the ropes, pulling the children to their feet, and together they marched through the camp.

21

A saddle had been strapped to the back of each elephant. A rope ladder extended to the ground, so the Emperor, his wife and their young children could clamber up each animal's side, and take their seat on its back.

Scarlett wasn't very happy about riding an elephant. Not only did she feel nervous, having never done it before, but she couldn't imagine that the elephant wanted to be ridden. Shouldn't an elephant be in the wild? Why had they been captured and brought here? Wasn't it cruel? She looked at Antonia and the others. If anyone else shared her worries, they hid it well.

'How did the elephants get here?' she asked

Antonia. 'This is an island.'

'How do you think?' Antonia replied.

'By boat?'

'You see? You're not so stupid! For a slave.'

Messalina had changed her stola and her hairstyle, and decorated herself with jewellery even more ornate, extravagant and expensive-looking than Antonia's. She was wearing thick gold bracelets on both arms. Around her neck she had a heavy gold chain, which lay on her chest like armour. Diamonds and rubies dangled from her ears. Even her two children, Tiberius and Octavia, had been dressed up with gold, silver and precious gems, so their faces and clothes glittered and glistened in the sunlight.

'Ah, Antonia,' Messalina said with a smile. 'You look lovely. Well done, my darling. You see? With a bit of hard work, anyone can be made to look beautiful. Now, that's your elephant – why don't you go and have a word with your driver, he'll tell you how to climb aboard.'

She pointed at the fourth and last elephant in the line, which somehow looked like the runt of the bunch, smaller, skinnier and less energetic than the others.

'Wait a minute,' Claudius called out. 'Let me see you.' He looked his daughter up and down, then nodded his approval. 'Perfect. Beautiful. Well done, darling.'

While Antonia had been getting dressed, her father had been inspecting the troops, making sure they were ready for the ceremony.

'You know what I told them? I said every scrap of armour must be polished so much that you can see your face in the metal like a mirror. The blade of every sword must be sharp. The tip of every spear must fill any onlooker with fear and terror as they imagine the metal breaking through their own skin, plunging into their guts, stopping their heart. Do you know why, Tiberius?'

'No, Daddy,' the little boy said.

'We have to put on a good show, my boy. These kings are brave warriors. They fight hard. Their island may be cold and dark. Their food might be nasty. Their lives are undoubtedly dismal and dreary. But they are still willing to give their lives for their wives, their children and their tribes. We have to convince them that they shouldn't even try. Resistance is useless! That's what they must think to themselves when they look at our steel, our men, our elephants. Our power. You understand me, little Tiberius?'

'Yes, Daddy,' the boy said.

'Good. One day, you'll be doing this too. When I'm dead.'

The little boy looked confused. 'Why Daddy dead?'

'Everyone has to die, but the empire will go on for ever. Once I'm gone, you will be the Emperor, and in turn, your son will inherit the power and the responsibility from you. Will you be a good emperor?'

'Yes, Daddy.'

'I'm sure you will.'

Aulus Plautius cleared his throat, then interrupted this chat between father and son, telling the Emperor that the eleven British kings were ready for him. The crowds were in their place. The soldiers had taken up their positions. It was time to board the elephants.

Claudius went on the first elephant. Next came his son, Tiberius, with two nurses – one sitting on either side – making sure he didn't slip out of his seat and fall to the ground. Messalina and Octavia took the third, leaving the fourth for Antonia and Scarlett.

A slave showed them how to climb aboard. 'Your foot goes here, my lady. Hold the rope with both hands. Then climb up. It's no different to climbing a ladder.'

Up at the top, the driver was waiting to guide them into their seats. Scarlett could see his face, peering down at them.

Antonia didn't hesitate for a moment. She might have been wearing a long dress, a woollen shawl and some very heavy jewellery, but she scrambled up the ladder as quickly and easily as if she was walking up a flight of stairs. Once she was safely sitting in the saddle strapped to the elephant's back, Scarlett climbed the same ladder.

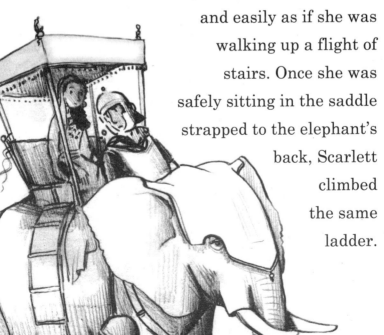

A little platform had been strapped to the elephant's back. There were two benches, one for the driver and another for the passengers, and a canopy to keep off the rain or sun.

Scarlett hadn't even had time to sit down when the elephant lurched forwards. If she hadn't grabbed the bench, she would have toppled off head-first, fallen down to the ground and been trampled under the elephant's enormous feet.

The four elephants took their places, lined up and ready to process through the camp. While they were waiting for the signal to start moving, Scarlett took the opportunity to ask Antonia a question: why had the Romans come to Britain?

'It sounds as if your father hates this country,' she said to the Emperor's daughter. 'His wife seems to hate it too. You don't seem to like Britain much either. Why have you come here? Why didn't your father just stay in Rome?'

'He needs an impressive military victory,' Antonia explained in low voice. No one would have been able to hear them but she was still cautious. 'My father is a wonderful man. He's loving, kind and generous, and very clever. But he's not strong. He doesn't look like a great leader. So he has to show he can conquer some territory.'

'Why did he choose Britain?'

'They're the worst savages in the world,' Antonia replied, not appearing to remember that she was talking to someone who, as far as she knew, was one of those very people. 'They're nasty, dirty and vicious. And utterly uncivilised. If he can conquer them, he must be a brilliant soldier. That's what the Senate and the people will think anyway, and the Emperor needs the Senate and the people to like and respect him.'

'What happens if they don't?' Scarlett asked.

'They plot against him,' Antonia replied. 'Maybe they even murder him. That's what they did to Caligula. And Julius Caesar. My father knows he'll probably get murdered too, that's just part of the job.' Antonia laughed, although she didn't really seem to be at all amused by what she was saying.

Imagine having a father who was not only the most powerful man in the world, but might at any moment be murdered by his enemies! Scarlett wouldn't have enjoyed that at all. She was much happier having parents like her own. Ordinary. Maybe a bit boring, but safe and secure and steady. They didn't have to look over their shoulders all the time, making sure that no one was trying to kill them.

'At last,' Antonia said.

Up ahead, one of the elephants trumpeted, and the procession started to move. Accompanied by rows of soldiers in glittering armour, they marched through the camp.

22

A huge crowd stood together, made up of locals from nearby villages, prisoners chained and roped together, and thousands of Roman soldiers preventing any trouble.

Standing apart from the others were eleven men (Thomas counted them), some accompanied by their families, others only by two or three soldiers.

All eleven of them looked magnificent. They were tall, strong, fierce warriors, dressed in robes, furs and armour. A few had tattoos on their arms, legs and even faces. Some of them were carrying swords, others had axes or spears, but none were wearing helmets.

'Who are they?' Thomas asked.

Bou was surprised that he didn't know. 'The kings,' she said. 'They've come here to give their surrender.'

'Why are they still armed? What if they started a fight?'

Again, Bou was surprised by the question. 'You can't take a man's weapons from him,' she explained. 'That is the worst humiliation possible. Any decent warrior would rather die than surrender his sword or his axe.'

Thomas didn't want to make himself look even more ignorant, but he managed to ask Bou some more questions, and she told him that they were eleven kings from different

tribes who controlled various parts of Britain. There wasn't a single king ruling over this island, and the different rulers often wasted their energy fighting one another. She said, 'If we could work together, we'd easily beat these Romans. Unfortunately, we've been fighting one another for so long, we can't stop.'

Bou didn't recognise every one of the eleven kings, but she knew most of their names and the territories that they ruled. 'He's Togidibnus, king of the Regni. Those two are the kings of the Corieltauvi, which they have divided between them. One of these days, they'll declare war on one another and see who gets the whole kingdom, but for now they have half each. That's the king of the Trinovantes. I can't remember his name. That's my husband, Prasutagus, king of the Iceni.'

Thomas wasn't sure he had heard correctly. 'Did you say he was your husband?'

'He's not actually my husband yet,' Bou

said. 'King Prasutagus won't marry me till I'm fourteen.'

Thomas remembered the name from their previous conversation. 'I thought you said he was a wimp and a coward?'

'He is.'

'Why do you want to marry a man who is a wimp and a coward?'

She looked at Thomas as if he was an idiot. 'No one cares what I want. My father has arranged the marriage to strengthen the bonds between our families and build the wealth of our tribe. I will have to marry him, whether I like it or not. But I'm going to make him miserable for the rest of his life.'

She giggled at the thought of the misery that she was going to inflict on poor Prasutagus.

Thomas couldn't help laughing too.

Some of the other prisoners standing nearby looked at them curiously, wondering what on earth those kids could find to laugh about at such a solemn occasion, but somehow their stares only made Thomas and Bou laugh even louder and harder.

The prisoners weren't the only ones to notice their laughter. They were also seen by some of the kings who were standing nearby, and some of their retinue, which included a tall man with a bushy auburn beard. He was staring at the two children as if he had never seen anything so extraordinary in his life. He spoke to the people around him, then hurried over.

'That's my dad,' Bou whispered to Thomas.

'Your dad?' Thomas couldn't believe it. 'We've been prisoners all day and your dad is here? Why didn't you get him to come and rescue us?'

'I'm not a baby. I don't need my dad to take care of me.'

As the man approached them, the Roman soldier Longinus stepped forwards, putting himself between Bou and her father. He didn't want anyone interfering with his prisoners.

In halting Latin, Bou's father managed to explain who he was.

'You can speak to her,' Longinus said. 'But you can't take her away. She's a terrorist, a rebel and a prisoner of the Roman army.'

'No problems,' Bou's father said in his bad Latin. 'I want speak with girl.'

Longinus stepped aside, but kept a wary eye on this Briton and the prisoners.

Bou's father looked at his daughter and shook his head. 'What are you doing here? I thought you were back at home with Mum.'

'Nice to see you too, Dad.'

'Come here.' He wrapped her in his arms and gave her a big hug. 'What's happened to you? Why are you a prisoner?'

Bou briefly explained how she had got into this position.

With every word that Bou spoke, her father grew more and more furious. 'I told you to stay at home with your mother and your brothers. She must be mad with worry about you.'

'Oh, she'll be fine,' Bou said. 'She'll just think I've gone hunting in the woods, which I had, but I wasn't hunting rabbits, I was hunting soldiers.' She giggled.

'That's not funny,' her father said.

He would surely have continued telling her off, but the crowd around them suddenly hushed, and Longinus told Bou and her father to do the same. The Emperor was arriving.

A troop of soldiers marched in first, followed by a huge grey beast with flapping ears and a long trunk. Three more beasts were behind it.

'Told you,' Thomas said.

Bou didn't answer. She and her father were staring at the elephants in silent astonishment. Neither of them had believed that such creatures could exist.

On top of the first elephant was a driver and a man in a white toga. That was Claudius, Bou's father told her and Thomas. The Emperor of Rome.

A little boy rode on the second elephant. He could only have been two or three years old, and was accompanied by a driver and two women, both dressed in simple tunics, so were probably nursemaids. That was what Bou's father said, anyway.

The third elephant was ridden by a woman and a young girl, and two older girls came on the fourth and final elephant.

The first elephant stopped. The Emperor sat there for a moment, looking at the crowds who had assembled and were waving at them. Then he stepped down the ladder to the ground.

Next came the little boy on the second elephant, who clambered to the ground, then toddled forwards, accompanied by his nurses. He looked around cheerfully at the soldiers, the prisoners, the kings and the nobles as if they had been brought here for his own personal amusement.

From the third elephant a little girl climbed down, accompanied by a young woman so elegant and beautiful that she drew the gaze of everyone gathered there in the camp. She walked slowly to the Emperor and stood by his side, her head

raised high, a haughty expression on her face.

Thomas was so entranced by the sight of this glamorous woman that he barely noticed the two girls who were riding on the fourth elephant.

Both of them were about his own age. For some reason, they were wearing very different clothes, one of them in a stylish dress and lots of glittering jewellery, the other in a simple tunic. He could see the face of one and only the back of the other's head, but even so he had the strangest feeling that he knew her from somewhere. Obviously that was impossible. He'd never been to the

year 43 before, and he didn't know anyone who had.

Except . . .

Could that be . . . ?

Thomas stared at the girl, willing her to turn in his direction. For what felt like a very long time, she looked the other way. Eventually one of the girls nudged the other, and they both turned to look at someone or something below them in the crowd, and for the first time, Thomas got a good look at their faces.

He couldn't believe it.

Here he was, miserable, cold and hungry, tied up with a metal collar round his neck and a rope securing him to a bunch of other kids, all of them forced to stand around for hours, guarded by bad-tempered soldiers who screamed at anyone who dared to step out of line – and meanwhile Scarlett was riding around on an elephant!

23

From her vantage point on top of the great lumbering beast, Scarlett could see a long way in every direction. The camp was much bigger than she had realised, packed with hundreds of tents and thousands of people. It was like a city.

A vast crowd had assembled to watch the ceremony, not only soldiers from the Roman army, but also prisoners who had been taken during recent battles, and thousands of locals from nearby farms and villages. They cheered the Emperor, oohed and ahhed at the elephants, and pointed out interesting sights to one another. There was a lot to look at. First came hundreds of soldiers, then the elephants, followed by a line of slaves, many of them carrying an amphora (a tall jar with two handles and a long neck) which Antonia explained had been filled with wine or olive oil, brought all the way from Gaul or Rome itself.

The elephants stopped in the middle of the crowd and the drivers helped their passengers to descend. The Emperor climbed down first, and took his position beside his generals. Next came his son and heir, the three-year-old Tiberius, accompanied by a couple of slaves. Messalina and her daughter came next, and finally Antonia and her own slave, Scarlett.

Eleven British kings awaited them, each accompanied by a few trusted advisers and close family.

Emperor Claudius issued an order to one of his soldiers, who called for silence.

'I have good news for you,' Claudius announced.

He spoke a sentence, then waited for his bilingual slave to translate his words for the British kings and the assembled crowd.

'You are now part of the greatest empire in the world.'

The eleven kings, their families, and the rest of the crowd listened in silence.

'You are not citizens, of course,' Claudius continued. 'You cannot expect the privileges that would be extended to a Roman. But you will be given the protection of the empire.'

Claudius told the local kings that they would each be allowed to rule over their own kingdoms, just as before. Only one thing would change: they would be more secure and comfortable because the Roman army would be keeping the peace.

'With our help, our guidance and our protection, you will be rich and happy, I can promise you that.'

Claudius announced that he was going to build a city right here where they were standing.

'This city will be the heart of Rome in Britain.'

He himself would be returning to Rome, he told them.

'I will be leaving my best general, Aulus Plautius, to rule in my place. He is appointed as governor of this new province. He acts with my authority. He speaks with my voice.'

Aulus stepped forward. He unfolded a piece of parchment and read the names of the kings, one by one.

'Togidibnus, king of the Regni.'

A tall man stepped forward. He was wearing a blue tunic and a long fur shawl. He walked to the Emperor, bowed, and said something in his own language.

Claudius greeted him, then Togidibnus stepped aside, and Aulus called the name of the next king.

'Dubnovellaunus, king of the southern Corieltauvi.'

A second man came forward. He was smaller than Togidibnus, but dressed even more grandly, wearing a yellow tunic, a bear skin over his shoulders, and a big gold medallion around his neck, hanging on a silver chain.

Aulus called the other kings one by one, and each

of them came forward to bow to the Emperor and pledge their loyalty to him and Rome.

'Volisios, king of the northern Corieltauvi.'

'Addedomarus, king of the Trinovantes.'

'Prasutagus, king of the Iceni.'

When all eleven of them had performed the same ceremony, Claudius presented them with gifts. He gave the same to each king: a bag of silver coins, a pair of gold bracelets, an amphora of wine and another filled with olive oil.

He turned to the soldier standing at his side. 'Now, we have prepared a little feast. Isn't that right, Aulus?'

'Yes, my lord. We have some wine and a few delicacies, fresh from Rome.'

'Bring them out, please.'

Some slaves brought cups, others carried amphorae of wine. Each amphora was as tall as Scarlett.

Claudius ushered the kings forward,

speaking to them, as always, via his translator. 'Come on, my friends. We have brought this wine from our vineyards on the hills around Rome. It has been aged for ten years. You will never taste a better vintage.'

Slaves poured out cups of white wine for the Emperor, his wife, and the eleven British kings. Together they drank a series of toasts, first to the Emperor and Rome, then to each other. Antonia took sips of wine too and joined in with the toasts, but no one offered a cup to Scarlett or any of the other slaves.

'I would like to propose a final toast,' Claudius called out, raising his glass. 'To friendship and mutual prosperity.'

Once the translator had explained what he was saying, the eleven kings repeated these words in their own languages.

'To friendship,' they called out. 'And prosperity.'

They drank and Claudius barked an order

at the slaves, telling them to keep the cups filled and bring out some snacks. Immediately slaves hurried forwards with large platters of delicious-looking delicacies: quails' eggs, cheese, olives, slivers of dried meat, cockles and mussels, radishes, carrots, bundles of herbs, piles of warm fresh flatbread and various other dishes that Scarlett couldn't identify.

Scarlett stood alongside Antonia, who sampled some of the dishes. The Emperor's daughter tried the cheese and the fish, then picked up a little round shell, and used her fingers to pry out the meat from inside.

'Those look like snails,' Scarlett said.

'That's because they are snails,' Antonia replied. 'Quite tasty ones too.'

She didn't offer Scarlett anything to eat, instead reaching for the contents of another tray carried by a different slave. 'Oh, give me one of those. Yum! I love roast thrush.' Picking up a tiny drumstick, she nibbled the meat, then threw the bone on the ground.

All this food made Scarlett so hungry! She wouldn't have been too keen to try the snails or the roast thrushes, but the bread, cheese, eggs and olives looked and smelled delicious. Unfortunately she knew she wouldn't get to eat anything, or not until later anyway, once the Emperor, his family and his guests had gorged themselves. If the slaves were lucky, they might be allowed to taste the leftovers when the feast was finished.

One of the British kings came up to Claudius. He bowed almost to the ground, then straightened up and had a word with the translator, explaining that he wished to speak to the Emperor.

When he heard this, Claudius blinked at the king. 'Who are you? I'm sorry, I know I've just heard your name, but I've forgotten it already. You all have such strange names, it's impossible to remember them all.'

'I am Prasutagus, king of the Iceni.'

'Oh, yes. So, Prasutagus, king of the Iceni, what do you want with the Emperor?'

'I beg your favour, my lord. I have a request for you. I beg you to release my wife-to-be, who, through some kind of mistake or accident, has been taken prisoner by your soldiers.'

'Your wife-to-be? Where is she now?'

'There, my lord.'

Prasutagus, king of the Iceni, pointed at the prisoners who were standing, chained and roped, on one side of the arena. Most of them were men, captured in battles over the past weeks. They would be sold as slaves and dispatched to different parts of the empire, where they would spend the rest of their days working, hundreds of miles from home, never seeing their families or friends again. Among the men was a group of children, and standing at the centre of them was a girl who couldn't have been more than ten years old.

When the Emperor and his family stared at her, the girl glared back defiantly.

Scarlett couldn't believe her eyes. She wasn't surprised by that girl, who she had never seen before. No, what she could not believe – what amazed her so much that she gasped out loud – was the boy standing beside her.

24

Thomas and Bou watched the ceremony together, seeing the Emperor and his general accepting the surrender of the eleven British kings.

Bou's father had returned to his place. He wasn't a king himself, but had come here as a trusted ally and adviser of his own lord, King Prasutagus. Now he stood with the rest of the Iceni, watching their allies and their enemies taking their turns to bow before the invader.

'Go on, Dad,' Bou hissed at him. 'Don't just stand there! Do something! Go and kill that emperor!'

'He'd never get away with it,' Thomas pointed out.

'That's not the point,' Bou replied. 'He'd die gloriously. What could be better than that?'

Thomas could think of a few things that were better than dying gloriously. Living comfortably, for instance. But he didn't say so, not wanting to sound like a coward.

Bou's annoyance only increased when the ceremony came to an end, and she saw King Prasutagus going over to the Emperor and speaking to him.

'Go on, fight him,' she hissed at her king and future husband. 'Challenge him to a duel.'

King Prasutagus couldn't hear her, but even if he had been able to, surely he wouldn't have followed her advice. He showed no sign of wanting to fight anyone, least of all the Emperor, instead bowing to him, then carrying on a lengthy discussion, mediated by a translator.

'Look at him,' Bou muttered, shaking her head. 'What a wuss.'

Soon a small group of Romans and Britons were walking in their direction: Emperor Claudius and his family, accompanied by King Prasutagus and his retinue, which included Bou's own father.

Along with the Romans and the British king, there was a girl in a neat tunic. Thomas wanted to shout out a greeting and ask what she had been doing, but he kept quiet, barely looking in her direction, not wanting to give any sign of the connection between them. Scarlett did the same. No one would have guessed that they had ever met before, let alone were brother and sister.

The Emperor peered at Bou. 'So, Prasutagus, king of the Iceni, this is your wife?'

'My wife-to-be,' Prasutagus replied. 'Her name is Boudicca. She is only young now, but we will be married when she reaches her fourteenth year.' He summoned one of the men standing nearby. 'This is her father.'

'Greetings, Emperor,' Bou's father said. He kneeled, prostrating himself before Claudius, and Prasutagus did the same.

'Thank you, thank you. No need for that. We're all friends here. Get up now.' Claudius ushered the two men back to their feet.

Boudicca had not kneeled, or even bowed. She wasn't intending to humiliate herself before the Roman Emperor, the invader of her country, however powerful he might be.

Prasutagus begged for the release of his future wife. 'She must have been taken prisoner by mistake,' he said. 'You have given us many generous gifts, Emperor, but I would swap them all for this one girl.'

Claudius wanted to know what had happened and how Boudicca had been taken prisoner. He asked Aulus Plautius to find out. Aulus summoned the troop commander who had captured her.

'She attacked us,' Longinus said. 'She and

her friends. They lay in wait for my men on a road through the forest.'

Boudicca's father promised that nothing similar would happen again. 'My daughter is young and foolish,' he said. 'She made a mistake, a very stupid mistake, and she has learned her lesson.'

Claudius turned to Longinus. 'She's only a child,' Claudius said. 'Are you really saying that she fought thirty of our men – and won?'

'No, my lord. She did not win. We overcame her easily. But she managed to cause some significant damage first.'

'Significant damage? What are you talking about? She's a girl! Did she scratch you? Pinch you?'

'They were armed with sticks, stones and slingshots, my lord.'

'Sticks and stones?' The Emperor laughed. 'You have swords, spears and shields. Or are you saying that you're not strong enough to fight a few girls?'

'No, my lord. Of course not. But she broke a man's nose. She might be young and small, and only a girl, but she's a fierce fighter.'

Claudius turned to Boudicca. 'I can see you're a fierce fighter for such a young woman. I have heard from your father and from your future husband. Now I would like to hear from you. So, tell me, are you sorry for what you did?'

'No,' Bou replied.

Her father and Prasutagus both started talking at once, but Claudius told them to be quiet. He wanted to hear from Boudicca herself. He asked her another question: 'Why

did you fight my men?'

Some people would have been intimidated by this situation, but not Boudicca. She stood up straight, looked the Emperor in the eye and replied with a question of her own. 'Why did you invade our country?'

'We haven't invaded,' Claudius said. 'We've come to free you from poverty and savagery. We are bringing civilisation to this wet, cold and depressing island. Your lives will be better now. We'll build roads for you. We'll show you how to live in the modern world. Trust me, you and your people will be better off as part of the empire than you ever would have been without us.'

'What if we don't care about being rich or having good roads or living in the modern world?' Bou said. 'What if we would rather be free, even if that means being poor?'

'Why would anyone want that for themselves or their children?'

'I would,' Bou replied proudly.

'You're a child. Wait till you're a bit older, you'll feel differently.'

'No, I won't.'

'Oh yes, you will. I can promise you that.'

Claudius smiled at Bou, not unkindly. He might have been patronising and condescending, but he was also generous. As the most powerful man in the world, he could afford to be. He turned to the king standing alongside him, and said, 'Are you sure you want to marry this girl, Prasutagus? She won't give you an easy life.'

'She is fierce, my lord. And proud. That is why she will not only make a fine wife for me, but a great queen for my people.'

'I admire your courage.'

Claudius ordered Longinus to set Boudicca free, along with the other children who had been captured after the ambush.

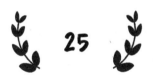

25

A steady stream of slaves hurried from the kitchens, carrying trays laden with delicacies: big bowls of olives which had been brought from Rome; sheep and chickens which had been found locally, slaughtered and cooked; chopped vegetables; white cheeses; boiled eggs; honey; more snails; more shellfish; more little birds which had been plucked and roasted; and other, even stranger foods that Scarlett did not recognise at all. Her hunger was so intense that she was practically fainting, but she still wasn't allowed to eat anything, and would have been punished severely if she had tried to snatch even a mouthful.

Messalina moved through the crowd, chatting to the kings and their families. Like Claudius, she was accompanied by a translator.

By this time, all the kings had drunk a lot of wine and were beginning to get rather tipsy. Some were giggling, others wrestled playfully and a couple burst into song.

Claudius called for more food and wine. Slaves filled everyone's cups, and brought round trays of apricots, figs, dates and grapes. The British kings had rarely tasted such delicacies, which didn't grow in their own country, and clustered around the slaves excitedly, wanting to taste everything.

After the feast, Claudius had laid on some entertainment for his guests, which began with a few songs performed by three young men with high voices. They sang in Latin, so the eleven kings couldn't understand the words, but they applauded politely at the end of each song.

The kings enjoyed the fighting much more. Five gladiators came out, fierce fighting men, barefoot, bare-chested, none of them allowed any armour or a helmet.

Each gladiator had been allowed to choose a single weapon. One had a sword. Another had picked a spear. A third had an axe. A fourth used a trident. The fifth and final man had perhaps been the last to pick his weapon because he was armed with nothing but a shield.

Claudius gave a little speech, wishing each of them good luck, then clapped his hands and the fighting began. The five men circled warily, waiting to see who would attack first.

The gladiator with the shield was the first to attack. He swung it through the air and smacked it into the head of another warrior, knocking him to the ground, then darted forward, and grabbed that man's weapon, an axe. The crowd roared their approval.

Scarlett was disgusted. It was horrible! How would anyone think that this was entertaining?

But they did. Both the British and the Romans appeared to be thrilled by the hand-to-hand combat. Claudius, Messalina and the British kings each chose their own favourites, and cheered on different gladiators, shouting encouragement at the tops of their voices.

Scarlett turned away and closed her eyes, but she couldn't block out the sounds of the fight: the thuds, the curses, the yelling and the screams.

Eventually the noise stopped. Scarlett opened her eyes. To her surprise, the winner was the gladiator who had only been armed with a shield. Blood poured down his face and chest, but he managed to limp over to the Emperor, who congratulated him and presented him with a few silver coins. The other four men lay on the floor, not moving, not even breathing.

As the celebrations continued, Antonia wandered through the crowd, peering at the British kings and their families, wanting to inspect these interesting savages. Scarlett stayed with her mistress, walking by her side, or a few paces behind.

When they passed Thomas, Scarlett took the chance to exchange a few words with him.

'You OK?' she asked in a low voice, not wanting anyone to suspect that they knew one another.

'Fine. All good. Only one problem. I don't have my device any more.'

'You lost it?'

'No, a soldier stole it from me, and smashed it. You'll have to help me get home, or I'm going to be stuck here for ever.'

A voice called to her in Latin. 'Scarlett! Come on!'

She looked around and saw her mistress beckoning impatiently to her.

She should have grasped Thomas's hand and pressed the button right at that moment, but before she had a chance to do that, he was jostled away from her by another slave.

'I'll come and find you later,' she called to her brother, then hurried after her mistress.

'Were you talking to that savage?' Antonia asked.

'He is from my tribe,' Scarlett answered. 'I was asking for news of my family.'

'Has he seen them?'

'No, my lady.'

Antonia nodded, not really interested in her slave's personal problems, and continued making her way around the eleven kings, having a good look at each of them. Scarlett accompanied her.

'Look at that!' Antonia tugged Scarlett's sleeve and drew her attention to some strange markings on one of the king's faces, swirls and dots painted in black, white and blue. 'Do you think he does that every morning or only on special occasions?'

Scarlett couldn't help giggling.

Later, a messenger arrived with a special announcement from the Senate in Rome. Horsemen had been riding day and night, passing this message from man to man, then crossing the sea in a boat, before bringing it here to the Emperor. The messenger unfolded a piece of parchment and read from the page.

'I bring a message from the Senate,' he said.

The message praised Claudius for his skill as a soldier and a statesman. He had succeeded in defeating some of the most ferocious, primitive and uncivilised tribes in the world. Only one previous Roman had come to this distant land and he, Julius Caesar, had retreated in failure. Only the great Claudius had succeeded in triumphing over the savage Britons.

It was lucky, Scarlett thought to herself, that

the British kings couldn't understand a word that was being said. If any of them had known Latin, they wouldn't have been too happy about hearing themselves and their country described in that way. Their translators understood every word, of course, but Scarlett noticed that they stayed quiet, not passing on the content of the letter to their masters.

From now on, the message concluded, Claudius would be known as Britannicus, as a reward for conquering this savage country.

Wild cheers greeted this announcement. Claudius bowed, accepting the adulation of his soldiers and fellow citizens, then waved for silence.

'I am grateful to the Senate for their praise, their kindness and their reward,' he announced. 'I am flattered by the new name that they have bestowed on me, but I shall not be using it myself. Instead, I am going to give this name to someone else. He is young now and has his life ahead of him. I know he will make better use of the name than me.'

He beckoned to his son.

Accompanied by one of his nurses, Tiberius toddled into the middle of the arena and ran to his father.

Claudius picked up his son, raised him into the air and addressed him in a loud voice, calling out his full name:

'Tiberius Claudius Caesar Britannicus!'

Cheers and applause came from the crowd.

Claudius continued speaking to his son, but his voice was loud and clear, obviously intended to be heard by everyone within earshot.

'Emperor Britannicus. Do you like the sound of that?'

'Yes, Daddy,' the boy said.

'You're going to be a good emperor, aren't you?'

'Yes, Daddy.'

'The greatest that Rome has ever seen?'

'Yes, Daddy.'

'I'm sure you will.'

Claudius deposited his son on the ground again, and then, holding his hand, led him forwards to meet the eleven British kings.

Scarlett thought it would be strange to have your name changed when you were three years old. You would just have got used to being called Tiberius, when you suddenly discovered that you were going to be called Britannicus from now on instead. Maybe emperors, and the children of emperors, were used to that kind of thing.

She was going to mention this to her mistress but when she turned around she realised that she was alone. Antonia had gone.

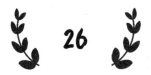

26

Bou stood with folded arms and a grumpy expression. She was being given a fierce lecture by her father. Thomas lingered nearby, eavesdropping on their conversation.

'What were you thinking?' Bou's father said. 'You and a bunch of kids against their soldiers – you didn't stand a chance! You could have been killed. You're lucky you weren't.'

'I had to do something,' Bou replied. 'I had to show them I don't want to be bossed around by a bunch of foreigners.'

'They're not going to boss us around,' her father said. 'Didn't you hear what the Emperor said? The Romans will let us be free as long as we trade with them.'

Bou laughed. 'Don't be silly, Dad. You can't trust the Romans. They'll say anything – they don't mean it.'

'I don't want you to get in any more trouble,' her father said. 'The Romans won't give you a second chance. Promise me this, Bou. No more fights. No more attacks on the Romans. Can you do that?'

'No.'

'I'm serious, Boudicca. You have to behave yourself, promise me you can do that. Otherwise they'll make you a slave, or even worse.'

Bou was furious. 'It's better to die honourably than live like a slave.'

'You can say that because you're only eleven years old. You'll think differently when you're an adult.'

'I won't,' Bou promised. 'I'll always hate the Romans.'

'When you marry Prasutagus, and you're

his queen, you'll have to pretend to like them, at least.'

'If I'm ever queen, I'll drive them out of my country.'

'Maybe you will,' her father said, 'but you'll have to unite all the different tribes first, not by fighting, but by making them work together. By persuading them to join you, fight alongside you and work together against their common enemy.'

'I can do that,' Bou said.

'I think you could,' her father agreed. He glanced around to make sure no one was eavesdropping on their conversation. 'But not today,' he continued, 'not when you're still a child, and not when you're alone. You're going to have to wait till you're a bit older, then you can unite all the tribes. Let them get to know you, get them on your side, earn their respect. Then they'll give their lives for you.'

'I can't wait that long,' Bou said. 'I want to

fight them now.'

'There's no point,' her father said. 'You'll die, and your death will be pointless. Wait till you're older, wait till you can command an army, then you can kick them out of our land. Will you do that?'

'I will,' Bou said. 'I promise.'

'What about your new friend? Will he help you?'

'I'm sure he will.'

'I'll do whatever I can,' Thomas said.

Bou's father arranged for the two of them to be taken away so they could wash their faces and put on some fresh clothes.

Thomas was given a clean tunic. He wondered if he would ever see his own clothes again. They weren't valuable or special, but Mum would want to know how he'd managed to lose a good pair of shorts and a reasonably new T-shirt and exchanged them for a very basic tunic made from a piece of old brown cloth tied with a piece of cord around his middle.

Boudicca had much nicer clothes; she was wearing a long white smock with a leather belt around her middle, decorated with intricate patterns. She was wearing jewellery too: silver earrings and bracelets, and a necklace of shiny green stones. Somehow the grubby kid who he'd met in the forest had been transformed into a princess. But her smile was still the same and so was the fierce expression in her eyes.

Not for the first time, Thomas wished he could bring her back to his own time. He'd love to see Bou in the playground, fighting the bullies, talking back to the teachers, mucking around with everyone, having the freedom to enjoy her childhood.

They joined the other kings at the feast, eating and drinking the delicacies that had been supplied by the Romans. Thomas stuffed himself with fresh bread and soft cheese, roast meat, boiled eggs, figs, grapes, plums and berries. It was all delicious. The whole feast was magnificent, a sign of the Emperor's wealth and generosity, and a promise of the good lives that awaited anyone who allied themselves with the empire. At the same time, the soldiers standing guard showed what would happen to anyone who chose a different path.

Thomas wanted to talk to his sister, and discuss how and when they were going to get out of here, but he couldn't see her anywhere. She had been standing near the Emperor during the ceremony, remaining by his side for the feast, and had been there during the strange moment when the Emperor swung his little son into the air and gave him a new name. But now, when half the people around here seemed to be drunk, and Thomas could finally have slipped away and talked to Scarlett, she seemed to have disappeared.

27

When Scarlett returned to her mistress's tent, she heard the sound of crying. Someone was weeping. But who? And why? In the back of the tent, she found Antonia with her head in her hands.

'What's wrong?' Scarlett asked.

'Nothing's wrong.' Antonia wiped away the tears, sat up straight and put on a tight smile, hiding all signs that she had been miserable. 'What are you doing here?'

'I came to see if you needed me, my lady.'

'I don't, you can go. Get some sleep. Come back first thing in the morning.'

'Yes, my lady.' Scarlett paused for a moment. 'Are you sure there's nothing wrong?'

'Nothing you can help with.'

'I could try,' Scarlett said.

'Could you improve the weather in this horrible country?'

'No, my lady.'

'Or the food?'

'No, my lady, but you won't have to endure it for much longer. You'll be going back to Rome soon.'

'That will be even worse.'

'I thought you liked it?'

'I love Rome,' Antonia replied. 'But as soon as we get home, I'm going to be married. Messalina has found a husband for me. She wants to get me out of the palace so she can have my father to herself.'

'Who are you marrying?' Scarlett asked.

'My first cousin. His name is Gnaeus Pompeius Magnus.'

'Do you like him?'

Antonia just laughed.

Scarlett wished there was something she could say or do to make Antonia feel better. Earlier that day, when she met the Emperor's daughter for the first time, she had thought Antonia was arrogant, spoiled and extremely annoying, but now she understood that she'd been wrong. Antonia was just very unhappy. She might have been the daughter of the most powerful man on the planet; she might have been so rich that she could have whatever she wanted; she might have owned a wardrobe full of fancy dresses and as many slaves as she needed; but, deep down, inside herself, she was just a depressed teenager with a horrible stepmother and a dad who seemed to have forgotten that she even existed.

Antonia must have grown to like Scarlett too, because she turned to her and said, 'I've made a decision. I was going to leave you here when I went home, you could have been a slave for Aulus. But I've got a better idea – I'm going to take you back to Rome.'

Clearly she expected her new slave to be overjoyed by this news, and Scarlett hoped that she managed to look sufficiently happy and excited. 'That's wonderful,' she made herself say. 'I'm so pleased, thank you! I can't wait to see Rome.'

'You're going to love it,' Antonia said. 'We have the best food in the world. Good weather too. And the buildings! Wait till you see the baths, the gardens, the forum, the Circus Maximus. You won't believe your eyes.'

Scarlett would have loved to go to Rome with Antonia, and for a moment, she imagined that she would. She pictured the seven hills circling the city, the senators in their togas, the chariots racing around the Circus Maximus and the other extraordinary sights and sounds that she would experience alongside the Emperor's daughter.

'We're leaving first thing tomorrow morning,' Antonia told her. 'My father has been on this foul island for almost two weeks. He says that's long enough for anyone to endure this terrible place. If the weather is good, and the horses are fast, we should be home in a month. I can't wait!'

'Me neither,' Scarlett said.

Without thinking, she wrapped her arms around Antonia and gave her a hug. 'Everything will be better when you get back home, I know it will.'

Antonia was shocked. Why was this slave hugging her? What if someone saw them? Then she must have realised that no one could see them, and no one would ever know what happened between them, because she hugged Scarlett back and whispered to her, 'Thank you.'

Scarlett held on for a long moment, then released Antonia and stepped away.

'I'll go and find Lucia,' she said.

'She'll be asleep.'

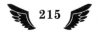

'I'll wake her up. If we're leaving in the morning, she and I will have to finish the laundry tonight and hang up your clothes, otherwise they won't be dry in the morning.'

Antonia smiled. 'You're clever, aren't you? For a slave. You can go and finish the laundry, but first you need to help me with my jewels. I can't take them off myself.'

'Yes, my lady.'

Scarlett helped Antonia to take off her earrings, necklace, bracelets and anklets, and store them in a wooden chest. If a thief ever managed to sneak into this tent, he or she would earn enough to live a very luxurious existence, but the Emperor's daughter always had six guards standing watch around her tent.

'Thank you, that's perfect,' Antonia said. She

washed her face, ready for bed, then brushed her teeth with an old stick dipped in a jar full of white powder.

'What's that?' Scarlett asked.

'Crushed oyster shells,' Antonia replied. 'It's the best thing to use if you want healthy white teeth.'

She walked to the door of the tent, spat through the gap, then handed her stick and jar to Scarlett to put away.

'You can go now,' Antonia said. 'Good night. See you in the morning.'

'Good night,' Scarlett replied. She put the jar and stick away, then slipped out of the tent, walked past the guards and hurried through the camp.

28

In the middle of the dark field stood a great pile of rocks, twice as tall as any man. Around them, the shape of a long rectangular building had been sketched out with ropes, showing the workmen where to dig foundations and start building walls.

One day, all these strong British rocks gathered from the surrounding fields and hauled up the hill, would be hammered into shape, fitted together and transformed into an enormous temple, a monument to Roman power and an offering to the Roman gods. But for now, they were just a bunch of big stones in the middle of a muddy field at the edge of the military camp.

On top of the pile sat two children, a boy and a girl, gazing into the gloom. On one side, they could see the lights of the camp, the candles and torches of soldiers who were still awake, and on the other the silhouettes of tall trees in the forest. Overhead, a perfect crescent moon hung in the clear sky, and the stars shimmered more brightly than Thomas had ever seen before; in his own time, the night skies were blotted out by lights from buildings and street lamps.

Thomas and Bou had been talking for ages. No one had come to disturb them. No one even knew they were here. They chatted about everything: their lives, their families, their ideas, their dreams.

Of course Thomas kept a lot from his new friend. He couldn't be absolutely honest, but he could still say a lot about his parents, his sister, his grandfather, and his own hopes and fears without admitting that he lived two thousand years in the future.

Bou told him about her life. She described her mother and two younger brothers, who had been left at home. She told him about her father, and the land that they owned, their house, their servants and her pet dog, a hound named River.

'I'd like to meet him,' Thomas said.

'You'd love him,' Bou said. 'He's the best dog in the world.'

She told him about Prasutagus too. She described the house where she would live and her duties as his queen. She was miserable and furious about the fate that awaited her, marrying a man who she barely knew and definitely didn't like.

'He did save you from being sold as a slave,' Thomas pointed out.

'You want me to be grateful to him?'

'I am. He saved me too.'

'We would have escaped,' Bou assured him.

'We didn't need rescuing.'

Thomas wished there was something that he could say or do to make his new friend feel better about her future, but he couldn't think of anything that didn't sound silly or irritating.

'I've been looking for you everywhere,' said a voice.

Thomas looked down at the ground and saw his sister standing at the base of the pile of rocks.

'Hi,' Thomas said. He turned to Bou. 'This is my sister.'

'Hello, Scarlett,' Bou said. 'Thomas has told me all about you.'

'Oh, has he? What did he say? I hope it wasn't anything too nasty.'

'He wasn't nasty about you at all,' Bou replied. 'He said you were the best sister in the world.'

'I don't believe that for a moment,' Scarlett said.

'You shouldn't because it's not true,' Thomas said. 'I actually just told her how annoying you are.'

'That sounds much more likely,' Scarlett said.

Bou laughed. 'Do you want to come up here?' she asked Scarlett. 'There's a great view.'

'I wish I could,' Scarlett replied. 'But he and I have to go.'

Sadly, Thomas got to his feet.

'It was great to meet you,' he said to Bou. 'Goodbye. And good luck.'

'You too.' She jumped up and gave him a hug. 'I hope we see one another again some time.'

'We will,' Thomas said.

He clambered down to the ground and joined his sister. Together they walked across the big field, ducking under the ropes and avoiding the trenches that had been dug in the damp earth. When they reached the nearest line of tents, they looked back at Boudicca.

She was still sitting on the top of the pile of rocks. She lifted her right hand and waved goodbye.

Thomas and Scarlett waved back.

'I wish she could come with us,' Thomas said.

'You know we can't do that.'

They continued walking through the camp until they found a shadowy place behind one of the tents where they couldn't be seen by anyone. Scarlett pulled the device out of the pouch hanging from her belt.

'Ready?' she asked.

'Ready,' Thomas replied.

He slipped his arm through his sister's, holding on tight. Scarlett pressed the button on her device. The wormhole sucked up the twins, spinning them through time and space.

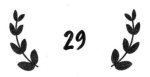

29

Back in the kitchen, Mum and Dad were beginning to get a bit annoyed.

They had come to Grandad's bringing lunch, but he didn't seem to be particularly grateful or even interested. In fact, he'd barely done more than say hello before disappearing into his workshop. First one of their children had gone to fetch him, then the other, but none of them had come back. Didn't they want any of this delicious lasagne? Or the garlic bread? Weren't they looking forward to the chocolate pudding and vanilla ice cream?

'What can they be doing in there?' Mum said.

'I'll go and fetch them,' Dad said.

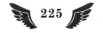

He left the house and walked across the yard to the workshop. He glanced at the notice pinned to the closed door:

```
DANGER
DO NOT ENTER
```

Dad knew the notice didn't apply to him. It was intended for the postie or any delivery drivers who turned up with a parcel.

He reached for the handle, but before he could grasp it, the door was flung open from the other side, and Thomas and Scarlett strode out into the bright sunshine, followed by their grandfather.

Dad burst out laughing. 'What's all this?' he said. 'Fancy dress? Where did you get all this stuff?'

Thomas and Scarlett stared at their father, their minds blank. Luckily their grandfather came up with an explanation.

'They wanted to try dressing up like the Romans,' Grandad said. 'Apparently it's something to do with their homework. I promised to help them. I'm so sorry, I know we're late for lunch, but we all got a bit carried away.'

'Oh, don't worry,' Dad said. 'It's all for a good cause. Come on, let's go inside and have something to eat.'

They arrived in the kitchen just as Mum was placing the lasagne on the table. It smelled amazing. She said, 'Who's hungry?'

'Me,' replied Scarlett, Thomas, and Grandad at exactly the same time.

HISTORICAL NOTE

The Romans first attempted to conquer Britain in 55 BC, when Julius Caesar landed with a large army. He stayed for only a few days before returning to Gaul (modern France) for the winter. He returned a year later and stayed for a few weeks, fighting and defeating some local tribes, before leaving again to put down a rebellion in Gaul.

In 43, almost a century after Julius Caesar's invasion, the Roman emperor Claudius sent another army to conquer Britain.

Claudius was born in 10 BC, became Emperor in the year 41, and ruled until his death in 54. He suffered various illnesses as a boy, which left him slightly deaf throughout his life. He was always weak and sickly; he stammered; and he walked with a limp. Assuming he could be neither a soldier nor a politician, he turned to writing instead, but he was, apparently to his own surprise, proclaimed Emperor after the assassination of his nephew, the Emperor Caligula, who ruled from 37 to 41.

As he does in this book, Claudius came to Britain after his general, Aulus Plautius, had conquered the native resistance. Claudius brought elephants to awe and intimidate the locals, and accepted the surrender of eleven British kings. (The twelfth, Caratacus, fled to Wales and hid there, launching more attacks against the Romans until he was betrayed by one of his allies and captured.)

Claudius ordered the construction of a

fortified town and a temple at Camulodunum, then left the island after only sixteen days and returned to Rome. His victory was celebrated by the Senate with a Triumph. The Emperor rode through the streets in a chariot, offered sacrifices at the temple of Jupiter and staged games and feasts for his grateful population.

Claudius had four children. He had a son, also named Claudius, who died at the age of three or four, then a daughter, Claudia Antonia, who appears in this story. She was born around the year 30. Her half-sister Claudia Octavia and her half-brother Tiberius Claudius were both about ten years younger than her.

Tiberius was given the name 'Britannicus' after Claudius's triumphant invasion of Britain. He was considered his father's heir, and therefore the future Emperor, until his parents divorced when he was seven years old. The following year, Claudius married

Agrippina the Younger, his fourth wife. She brought a son, Lucius, from a previous marriage. Lucius would later be renamed Nero, marry his step-sister Claudia Octavia, and become Emperor after the death of Claudius.

A few days before his fourteenth birthday, Britannicus attended a grand dinner with his sister and his stepmother. He was given a hot drink. He asked for some cold water to bring down the temperature. There was poison in the cold water, and after taking a sip, he collapsed, unable to breathe, and died. No one knew for sure who poisoned him or why, but at the time it was assumed that he had been murdered by his step-brother Nero to prevent him from ever trying to become the Emperor himself.

Claudia Antonia's life wasn't much happier than her half-brother's. Only a few months after the Roman invasion of Britain, she was married to Gnaeus Pompeius Magnus, the son of a wealthy Roman nobleman. When he died, Antonia married his half-brother, Faustus Sulla. They had a son, who died when he was still a toddler. Faustus Sulla himself was murdered on the orders of Nero.

Nero had been married to Antonia's younger sister, Claudia Octavia. He divorced her, then murdered her and married again. After his second wife died, Nero asked Antonia to marry him. When she refused, Nero had her executed.

We know a lot about the Romans, because they wrote about themselves and many of their works have survived. (Claudius himself wrote about forty books, although sadly not a single one still exists.) Unfortunately, we know much less about the people who they fought against and conquered, because they left so few records of their own lives, deeds or thoughts.

We only know about Boudicca through the writings of two Romans, Tacitus and Cassius Dio. Both of them were writing many years after she died. There is no archaeological evidence that she even existed, nor any other descriptions of her life or battles. No one really knows exactly where or when she was born, although she probably was about ten years old when Claudius invaded Britain in 43. Even her name is uncertain, not just its spelling – which might be Boudica, Boudicca, Boadicea, Boudicea, or Buddug – but also whether it was even her actual name or simply a title meaning 'victory' or 'victorious'.

According to Tacitus and Cassius Dio, Boudicca married King Prasutagus, the ruler of the Iceni, who lived in what is now East Anglia. King Prasutagus made a treaty with the Romans, agreeing to hand over half his kingdom to them when he died on the condition that his and Boudicca's two daughters could keep the other half. After his death, the Romans ignored their previous agreement and took the whole kingdom for themselves. Infuriated by this treatment, Boudicca roused her tribe into rebellion and raised a large army, hoping to drive the Romans out of Britain.

The current Roman governor, Gaius Suetonius Paulinus, was fighting in Anglesey, an island off the Welsh coast, and had left his towns and cities without adequate protection. Boudicca attacked the Romans in Camulodunum and burned the whole place to the ground, destroying the military camp, the city and Claudius's temple. She marched her army to London, destroyed that city too, then did the same to St Albans (Verulamium).

By this time, the governor and his own army were returning from Anglesey. Boudicca marched to meet them. According to Tacitus, the battle was an overwhelming victory for the Romans, who lost only 400 men, whereas 80,000 Britons were killed.

Cassius Dio says that Boudicca died of her wounds after the battle. According to Tacitus, she took poison to avoid being captured.

After Boudicca's death and the massacre of her army, the Romans reinforced their camps and towns, built temples, villas and roads, and stayed in Britain for several centuries, not leaving until around the year 410.

After Boudicca destroyed Camulodunum, the Romans moved their British capital to London. Stroll through the centre of London, and you will see a large statue of Boudicca, waving a spear and driving a chariot with two horses. Although this statue isn't exactly historically accurate, it's very evocative. Stand nearby, and you'll find yourself imagining how this place might have looked two thousand years ago. You'll see crackling flames, and smell the burning buildings, and hear the shouts of Roman soldiers fleeing from Boudicca's army.

The Romans rebuilt the city of Camulodunum and gave it a new name, Colonia Claudia Victricensis, which means 'the city of Claudius's victory'.

Camulodunum is now called Colchester. If you visit the town today, you can see the remains of some Roman walls and the foundations of the Roman temple, which was converted into a castle by the Normans.

It is now a museum where you can see many fascinating exhibits, including a beautiful model of the temple of Claudius, along with Roman coins and dice, pots and jars, weapons and armour, and even the metal hoops that would have been placed around the necks of their prisoners.

ACKNOWLEDGEMENTS

The story in this book was inspired by visiting Colchester Castle. I wandered among the foundations of the temple, and strolled through the museum, looking at the amazing exhibits on display, and ideas and characters bubbled into my imagination. I'd like to thank everyone who works at that museum, and the staff of the British Museum and the Museum of London. Please do visit these museums if you get a chance – or you can explore their collections online.

I have also been inspired by visiting Roman sites throughout Italy and Britain, and by reading many wonderful books about Boudicca and the Romans, from earnest histories to *I, Claudius* and *Asterix the Gaul*. I'd like to thank all the writers, archaeologists, historians and artists who have uncovered, illuminated and interpreted the history of the Romans in Britain and of the local inhabitants who fought, welcomed or simply endured these invaders.

I'd also like to thank the people who made this book with me. Thank you to everyone at Andersen Press, particularly my editors, Eloise Wilson and Charlie Sheppard. Thank you, Garry, for your wonderful illustrations.

Finally, my thanks and love to Bella, Esther, Rosie, and Pippi.

TIME TRAVEL
TWINS

THE
VIKING
ATTACK

JOSH LACEY
ILLUSTRATED BY GARRY PARSONS

Twins Scarlett and Thomas are
struggling with their history homework,
until Grandad comes to the rescue with
his time machine. Suddenly it's 859 AD.

Thomas is catapulted on to a Viking
longship full of wild warriors sailing
to attack an Anglo-Saxon village. But
Scarlett lands in that village, and meets
a young Alfred the Great, who will do
anything to defend his country against
the bloodthirsty invaders . . .

TIME TRAVEL TWINS
THE
VIKING
ATTACK
JOSH LACEY
ILLUSTRATED BY GARRY PARSONS